MW00768122

-24

Sonny

a novel

Jewel Pierce

HATS
OFF

Sonny

Published by Hats Off Books™
610 East Delano Street, Suite 104, Tucson, Arizona 85705 U.S.A.

www.hatsoffbooks.com

International Standard Book Number: 1-58736-289-9
Library of Congress Control Number: 2003099675

This book is lovingly dedicated to my husband,
Harold Hunter Pierce, Ph.D.

As was so often the case, Weeda McVey had worked late and except for Mr. Drago, the principal, was the last staff member to leave the building. One-on-one counseling sessions had filled the day, pushing the record keeping and telephone contacts to after-school hours. Time wise, this day had been no different from yesterday or the day before. What had blasted the otherwise sameness was the bombshell Sonny Houston had dropped during sixth period. How could or should she deal with what she had been told? How could Cody Houston, Sonny's dad, a church elder and a very influential leader, have pulled off such a thing?

As she walked toward the parking area, she tried to filter out some of the confusion. Maybe she had fallen asleep and dreamed this wild tale. Glorious thought but only in fantasy! A few minutes later, she was jarred into reality when she noticed her gas gage was on empty.

Immediately she headed for the closest service station—the Gulf—on Pendleton Street. As she was parking, a Buick LeSabre pulled in behind her. In the rear-view mirror, the driver looked like—was it who she thought it was? Almost as if by instinct, her head went down as though trying to retrieve an article from the floorboard. She could not risk coming face to face with Mr. Houston, not today. Though as a counselor she had been trained to conceal and stifle her reactions, she didn't think she was poker-faced enough to hide her thinking, much less her feelings.

Surely her eyes would belie her otherwise controlled tongue. She certainly did not want to strike up a conversation with the man so soon after what she had learned about him. Without further thought, she cranked up and sped away. Hopefully, she'd have enough fuel to make it to the GP station on the road to Dellisville.

Kyle Sanders closed his office at 6:30, relieved that the day was over. Now he could look forward to a quiet evening at Weeda's place. Every so often she opted to cook in lieu of the once-a-week dine out. He had been seeing her for about three months and their dating was becoming routine: dinner once a week, church on Sunday evening except when he was on call, and time together for special occasions. He wasn't sure where their relationship was headed, if anywhere, but he was certain of one thing: as of now he wanted it to continue.

At his Elms Street apartment, he showered, shaved, and was donning a khaki outfit when the telephone rang. "Hi Kyle, this is Weeda. I'm sorry. Something has come up and I have to renege on my dinner offer. Nothing physical or personal, just some school 'pop ups' surfaced this afternoon. Hopefully, I'll be seeing you this weekend."

After she reassured him that school concerns were the basis for the cancellation, he hung up. A few minutes later he was scrounging around in the kitchen trying to find something to satisfy his hunger and mollify his disappointment. He layered some cold cuts—ham, cheese, lettuce, and tomato—into a sandwich and downed it with a glass of cold milk, then stretched out on the lounger expecting sleep to take over, but winding down came slowly. A semi-satisfied dissatisfaction prevailed, having mostly to do with Weeda's breaking the date. What, he wondered, had happened at Rushton Christian School that was so disruptive?

"Oh well," he said, half-aloud, "Who am I to complain about interruptions and cancellations?" In his thinking, that was expected in the life of a doctor. But it was not supposed to be so for school personnel. Their schedules were designed to be reasonable and predictable, or so he thought.

* * *

Weeda couldn't sleep. Repeatedly, just as she was about to drift off, the thought of Sonny Houston's dilemma punctured her otherwise dozing consciousness and she was alert again.

"Oh Lord," she prayed, "help me to fall asleep and be unto me as you were unto the Prophets of Old; give me a dream informing me how to handle this situation, and if the dream is rendered in symbols, upon awaking, may I be given, as was Joseph, an interpretation of the dream. Thank you, Lord."

* * *

The following Friday, Sonny was back in the guidance office. As always, he was neatly dressed, his hair tousled just enough to give him that playful look, but his blue eyes were missing their usual merry glint and for good reason. He was perplexed. He needed help in sorting through his emotions.

"Sonny," said Ms. McVey, "You were so upset when you were here the other day. You told me what you had discovered but didn't tell me how the discovery came about, and I've wondered."

"Well, I'm not sure I can remember the straight of it. It was Saturday morning, and I was covering for Dad at the office. He pays me to do that some Saturdays cause Houston Enterprise employees work just five days a week. I like the money and it's not hard, just answering the phone and that kinda stuff."

"So you were there alone?"

"Right, and at about eleven, Dad called and said he had been delayed outside town and for me to lock up at noon and be sure everything was secure. When I went to lock the file cabinets, I noticed the lower drawer of the third cabinet was ajar. I was surprised 'cause that file has its own separate lock and nobody has a key except Dad, not even Ms. Sheldon, the secretary. Well, when I pulled on the handle, out it came. It was pretty much like all the other files, just not as packed. I was about to slam it shut when a folder marked 'ADOPTION' caught my eye. For a minute, I couldn't catch my breath. As everybody knows, I've always been happy about my adoptive parents, but specifics about my real parents do cross my mind, and that was my first thought: 'My adoptive records are in that folder.' Sure enough, there they were, but I was not prepared. I thought I was going to pass out. The who and how sent my mind reeling, and I'm still reeling."

"I can imagine, but these findings could bring you and your dad even closer."

"When the shock wears off, maybe I'll see it that way."

"After thinking about it for two days, have you come to a decision about what you'll do, if anything?"

"No, that's why I've told you. I can't sleep, I can't eat, and I'm afraid the folks will notice. What should I do? Keep it to myself or let them know I know?"

"Well, you're 18, and a mature 18 I might add. I think the best way I can help you is to discuss your options—the pros and cons of keeping your findings secret or sharing what you've found out."

"What I don't understand is—well, even if I could accept it all, some people if they knew would want him run out of town. Everybody knows I'm adopted. That's no secret, but I wonder what the fallout would be if they knew what I know?"

"Do you suppose some people know but have kept silent?"

"Beats me. I sure don't think Mom knows. If she does, she's—well, I can't believe she does. I wish I knew what to do."

"I wish I could be as King Solomon to you, but I'm minus his gifts. You have two choices: keep your discovery to yourself and hope this knowledge won't adversely affect your attitude toward your dad, tarnishing your close and loving relationship, or share what you know and go from there."

"Yeah, I know. If I keep quiet, it's gonna eat on my mind and I can't be myself."

"That's true, and that insight will probably provide the answer you're seeking."

"You mean I ought to tell him?"

"I mean it's going to be hard for you to pretend. You're real, not a fake, and that warm and open personality just might become tarnished through pretense. Think about it. I have a meeting in ten minutes. If you want to talk some more on Monday, I'll be here."

"Thanks, Ms. McVey, for listening to me."

"Sure." As Sonny ambled toward the door, she added, "Sonny, has it occurred to you that maybe, just maybe, your dad purposely unlocked that drawer and left it ajar?"

* * *

The late October afternoon was just right for strolling, so Weeda and Kyle walked from her place to the Big Tree on Principal Avenue to have a snack before church.

Kyle ordered crab soup for himself and a cottage-cheese fruit salad for Weeda. While they were waiting to be served, Kyle mentioned the dinner cancellation. "Did you get the Wednesday's 'pop-up' school problem solved?"

"Well, no, but we're still talking."

"Anything about it you want to discuss?"

"I suppose I can't. It's like some of the things that come through your office. You're ethically bound to silence."

"I understand that."

"The difference is that you deal with the physical, and though much of my work is focused on academic and personal planning, there are times when emotional and spiritual bombshells fall my way, and it really gets rough and sticky, especially when prominent and influential leaders are entangled."

"A thorny situation, eh?"

"Very. Does it bother you to distraction when you learn about people here in Rushton—detrimental things that if publicly known would jeopardize their standing with their families, the church, and the community?"

"It concerns me, but I just have to pretend I don't know."

"That's for certain, but in this case a much-needed resolution could bring the exposure of influential people and I'd be right in the middle of it."

"Sounds as though you've been worrying about this."

"To tell the truth, I have. I don't like knowing what I know. Makes me vulnerable."

"To what?"

"I'm not sure; I just feel uneasy."

"Job wise, safety wise, or what?"

"I hope I'm not borrowing trouble. It's possible you have knowledge of this situation."

"I doubt it. Why don't we pray about it after church tonight? Here's our food."

They were quiet while driving back to Weeda's place after church. Weeda finally broke the silence. "Kyle, when the evangelist talked about some people being taken and some being left, what did he mean? Who's who? Is it the saved who are being taken or is the other way around?"

"I don't know at this point, but I think I'll make an effort to find out. Like so many other ministers when dealing with the prophetic, he threw out conflicting viewpoints and theories. Such sermons give the believer the freedom to choose the scenario that makes him most comfortable, I suppose."

"I must say I am confused."

"You're saying you don't know which theory to believe?"

"Well, yes, I suppose that's what I'm saying. It's like taking a multiple-choice test."

"Exactly, and I don't think God intends for us to have choices concerning the truth of His word. As I sat there tonight, I made a decision to find out what God Himself has to say about His church as related to the end of the age."

"You're going to find out? How? Where will you go for the answers?"

"Weeda, dear, the same resources available to the preachers are available to you and me. I don't wear a clerical robe or my collar turned backward, but I can read; I can pray; and I can seek the help of the Holy Spirit."

"Wow! You are serious. You already spend more time in Bible study than most laymen. Pray tell, where will you find the additional hours?"

"I'm making that a matter of prayer. But as you are my witness, I'm making a commitment to study these theories that are so confusing to so many Christians. Want to join me in the endeavor?"

"Oh my, I'll have to think about that. Maybe I should settle for something more suitable to my Christian size—such as supporting you in prayer. You do the studying, and I'll learn from you."

"Not a bad idea. I'll need a sounding board."

At the door as they said goodnight, Weeda asked, "Will I be seeing more or less of you now that you're becoming a scholar of biblical studies?"

"That, my dear, is up to the Lord, but I hope it won't be less."

Kyle drove home slowly, his mind not on his driving but on the conversation he had just had with Weeda—about how his decision to delve into a study of eschatology had seemingly been an instant impulse. Or was it so sudden? Hadn't he from time to time pondered on these end-time theories? The suddenness aside, not since he resisted his father's insistent demands that he come into the family business fifteen years ago had he been so sure he was setting his aim in the right direction. Something in his spirit was registering an affirmative nod, the same assurance he had experienced when as a college senior he had announced to his father that he planned to study medicine. Highly displeased, Daddy Sanders tried to make life unpleasant for him, but his efforts failed. Seven years later he began his specialized practice in internal medicine.

Reveries of the past kept tumbling down. Did he have regrets? No, because intuitively he knew he had trod the path God had wanted him to take. Later, that same gut feeling had come over him when he decided to investigate the merits of prayer counseling, which had interested him because he had seen how this ministry had made a difference in the lives of some of his patients. Now again he felt that same spirit of commitment nudging him concerning Bible prophecy. How could he fit more study into his schedule? He didn't know, but he knew that he would. He would endeavor to give to this topical study the quality time he had previously devoted to the study of prayer counseling.

* * *

A short time later, while Kyle was peacefully falling asleep, Weeda was tossing and turning trying to enter slumber land but to no avail. Kyle's declared determination to become even more of a Bible scholar, though commendable, had disturbed her. She valued the fact that she and Kyle shared a Christian faith. It gave them common interests, goals, and a meeting of the minds. He understood her decision to work at a Christian school even though the pay was less and the benefits fewer than she could have had in the public schools. Christian affiliations were important to him and he was certainly a seven-days-a-week Christian, not of the Sunday-only ilk. Then why was she anything but pleased that he was committing himself to this endeavor? She couldn't explain the uneasiness but she recognized it. If his findings led him to doctrinal views that differed from those of the church leaders, would he take issue with the ministers or maybe the elders? Where would she fit in? She should be thrilled, but she wasn't.

* * *

Mrs. Larson, the guidance secretary, buzzed Weeda's phone.

"Yes, Mrs. Larson?"

"One of your regulars is here."

"Which one?"

"Hammie Hanks. He says he has to talk to you right away. He has a detention slip, and this is his study period."

"Oh my! Tell him to come on in."

Hammie ambled in and leaned against the wall just inside the door.

"Haven't seen you in several days. Have a seat."

"I don't wanna set no more. I been settin' all day, and it ain't over yet. Looks like I'll be settin' in the Big D after school."

"In detention? For what reason?"

"Well, it's that same English teacher. Ever time sumpin goes wrong she thinks I done it or if she knows good and well I didn't do it, then she thinks I know who did do it."

"Ms. Rhymer, huh? Tell me what happened."

"Well, somebody put a squeaky toy under the seat cushion of her chair so when she plunked her bottom down—well, she didn't like what she heard, but everybody else did." Inwardly, Weeda had a twinge of amusement but managed to keep a straight face.

"So she thinks you put it there?"

"Well, that's how she let on. But that's not all. When I told her I had nothing to do with it, she got right up in my face and used words nobody knowed what she wuz talkin' 'bout, least I didn't. She said I wuz always doin' sumpin to get attention and she just kept sayin' she knowed I done it—said her instinct told her so. And she really got mad when I told her my end stinks too but it don't tell me nothin'. That's when she blowed her top and give me this here slip. I don't know what I done wrong. I see you're laughin' too. I can't see what's so bad 'bout makin' people laugh now and then. It's better'n makin' 'em cry."

"You don't understand why your comments—what you said—made her angry?"

"That's what I'm tryin' to splain. And besides that, she called me names. Said 'you're obscene' or sumpin lack that. I told her I didn't know who she was talkin' 'bout. I've never heard of Ob, much less seen him. But whoever he is, he must be somebody she thinks is really bad."

Weeda was too amused to be angry. She explained as best she could the meaning of the words and he seemed to comprehend. At the same time, she was scribbling and making notes.

"Now Hammie, take this pass along with this note to study hall where Ms. Rhymer is in charge. Tell her you now know why she was angry and ask her to forgive you. You know how to do that."

"I ought to. I get plenty practice. Seems lack I never get through 'pologizin. I'm thinkin' the kids might start callin' me 'Apostle Ham'."

"Well, again it's the right thing to do, and it might get you off that Big D list."

"I'll give it a try." As he was going out the door, he turned, shrugged his shoulders and in his twangy voice said, "Beats me. I sure do step in it with that woman."

After Hammie left, Weeda was preparing to wind things down for the day when the buzzer sounded again.

"Macy Bryant is here and hopes you can see her this period. What shall I tell her?"

"I can arrange to see her, but hold on. I'm checking her schedule. She's a cheerleader, and this is their special practice period. I don't like students cutting other activities if it can be avoided. Remind her of this unwritten rule and buzz me back."

She continued to tidy up her desk, sorting papers and folders into priority baskets. To herself she said, "I wondered how long it would be before she came into the picture. Maybe this has nothing to do with Sonny Houston, but then I'm suspicious that it does."

"Ms. McVey, Macy says she'll go to practice and see you during third period tomorrow."

"OK. Write her a pass and I'll see her then, and I'm going home as soon as the bell rings, so I'm not available for any after-school work."

"That's unusual. Are you all right? Anything wrong?"

"No, I'm making dinner for a friend and need some extra time to brush up on my domestic and culinary efforts. See you tomorrow."

That night she and Kyle enjoyed their dinner from trays in front of the TV and watched World News Tonight. Kyle ate quietly but heartily of the stuffed peppers, red rice, and garden salad. It was intriguing to note how completely absorbed Kyle was in the reports, seemingly oblivious to her presence. She questioned how he could be so taken up with such things when there were other concerns that, in her mind, needed immediate consideration. It was amazing how he could concentrate on one thing at a time even in the midst of chaos and confusion. When he was in the office, it was all medicine; when at church, it was the Bible and the interpretation of it; when he was fishing, he was outsmarting those scaly little swimmers; and when he listened to the news, his mind was on current events and the people who did the reporting. Why, she thought, couldn't *she* have more of that purposeful singlemindedness? At school, she often found herself mulling over personal and past experiences; at church her mind wandered back to school matters. But not Kyle.

Peter Jennings was bidding his usual goodnight so she muted the sound and was about to mention his total absorption with the report when he interrupted her thoughts: "You're a gifted person, you do know?"

"Me? In what way?"

"In many ways. In evidence here tonight is your knack for putting tasty food together in the right combinations."

"Well, thank you, but I don't see anything unusual about that. Cooks the world over do it every day."

"Oh yeah? You obviously haven't eaten at some of the places I have. But enough of that. Did you get that thorny school problem resolved—the one that stole our last dinner date?"

"You sound as though you're still a bit teed off about that cancellation."

"No, not really, but I was disappointed. Are things working out for your counselee?"

"No, it's still ongoing, but for the time being he has made a decision to remain quiet and keep things confidential, so developments are on hold and that suits me. Maybe he'll hold off 'til next year, and possibly I could avoid the whole problem by transferring to another position."

"My! That's a drastic step just to help a client."

"It might be the only way I can avoid taking on a problem for myself—one to which I couldn't find a solution. If the boy should choose to talk, well, that could open up the proverbial keg of worms, and I'm afraid they'd be crawling all over the place—in the school, in the church. At her request, I'm seeing his girlfriend tomorrow. Whether her need has any connection to his recent dilemma, I don't know. Surely not, if he's as closedmouth as he appears to be."

"Don't bet on that closed mouth. Don't assume his problem is a secret between the two of you. Very few people confine their confessions to only one confidant."

"I'll bear that in mind. Are you making any headway on your Endtime studies?"

"Sure am. In fact, I've already purchased some resource materials, and Saturday, instead of going fishing, I'll be studying. I'm trying to decide just where to begin and have been talking with some of my patients who know the Scriptures. They suggest starting with Daniel. I don't quite see it that way. In his Olivet Discourse, Jesus made some definite statements about His return, so I'll start with Matthew 24 and see how all the other prophetic passages tie into those verses. I expect to find zero contradictions. Since the Holy Spirit is the author of all Scripture, these truths, coming from the same source, should fit together like hand in glove.

"That makes sense, but something I would never have reasoned out. Remember, I'm your sounding board. In that way, I get the benefits without all that effort."

"I'll be glad to accommodate. Now after I help you do the dishes, I'd better scoot. I have to start my hospital rounds at seven, bright and early."

* * *

Weeda's morning had been full, but not so jammed packed that it had blocked out the dread of seeing Macy Bryant. Third period had just begun, and she was ready to delve into whatever it was Macy had on her mind. About that time, Ms. Larson buzzed, saying Macy was in the waiting area.

"Good. Tell her to come on in."

When she entered, Weeda was scanning Macy's folder as if to relay the expectation of discussing academic concerns. "Hi there; I haven't seen you to talk to you in quite some time, but I do enjoy watching your acrobatics at the games. You and the cheerleading team are really good."

"Thanks; we work at it, and it's fun."

"Looking at your record here, I see you're carrying a heavy load—four college prep courses plus journalism, two clubs. Do you have any time to play?"

"Cheerleading for me is play." Her bright eyes were dancing as she said it. She was a lovely young thing: a flawless creamy complexion and classic roman profile with features all in proportion. Her oval-shaped face enabled her to wear her hair in a variety of styles. Loosely on her shoulders, she looked girlish, but when pulled back in a bun, she had the appearance of a sophisticated grown up. If anything was troubling her, it was not being reflected in her demeanor.

"Ms. McVey, I'm not here to talk personal planning. I'm here on behalf of a friend."

"Oh?"

"It's my boyfriend, Sonny Houston. I wish he'd come in to see you. Something is wrong and he won't tell me what it is."

"Is it something you suspect or has he indicated as much?"

"I questioned him and he admitted he was worried but wouldn't talk about it."

"Do you have an inkling?"

"Not really. But I'm wondering if he has an urge to find out about his birth parents."

"Why do you say that?"

"Well, more than once he's mentioned how breaking the genetic code makes him wonder about some things—how I'm lucky that I know who my ancestors are."

"Are you concerned that he is adopted?"

"No, not really, except that worrying about it might affect him in a negative way. I was wondering if you might call him in to discuss his records and in that way give him an opportunity to open up. He regards you highly."

"I appreciate your saying so, but I'll have to give your suggestion some thought. I prefer that students initiate their own appointments when it comes to personal problems. In the meantime, maybe you could just openly ask him about what you suspect."

"Maybe so, but I have a feeling he thinks I'm being too nosey, probing too much."

"I appreciate your sharing with me Macy, and I think it's commendable that you're interested in Sonny's concerns, but why not give him a little more time, and in the meantime, I'll give some consideration to your suggestion."

* * *

The following Tuesday, Sonny was back in the counseling office looking pensive.

"Well," asked Ms. McVey, "have you made a decision, that is, about whether to discuss your findings with your parents?"

"No, not completely, but I'm leaning toward keeping it quiet. I've thought and thought—not just about myself but what affect this might have on Macy. I mean on our relationship. If things don't work out for us, I want it to be because we're not right for each other."

"But she knows you're adopted so obviously that's not a factor for her."

"That's true, but to her my birth parents are unknown."

"You're thinking that when your relationship is more settled, she can make better judgments—put things in perspective?"

"Right. We haven't been dating too long, so we're just getting to know each other. When she knows how she really feels about me then she'll be in a better position to decide whether my background really matters. Whew! I'm confused. Am I making sense?"

"I understand. You're saying that if she rejects you, you want the rejection based on your personal attributes."

"That's right. I'm afraid to factor in this bombshell at this time."

"Sounds as though you're serious about Macy."

"Well, she's different, that's for sure, and I like that. Do you think I'm doing the right thing by staying quiet?"

"I doubt if it's a matter of what's right and what's wrong. It's not that simple. Seems to me it's a matter of whether you want to wrestle with concealment or with exposure. Either way, there is some grappling ahead for you."

* * *

Shortly after classes were dismissed for the day, Weeda's phone rang. It was Mr. Drago. "Ms. McVey, can you break away and come to my office?"

"Oh my!" she thought, "I was planning to check out a bit early," but to her boss she replied, "Yes, Mr. Drago, do I need to bring any records or reports?"

"Yes, bring whatever you have on Hammie Hanks. His father is here about another of Hammie's conflicts. I doubt if academics will enter in the picture, but bring the records anyway. Hopefully, we won't be long."

Weeda knew how unpredictable time wise those parental conferences could be, so she ambled down the hall while pondering. Half-aloud, she wondered what Hammie had done this time. In spite of the note she had sent to Ms. Rhymer concerning the squeaky toy incident, Hammie had not been excused from the detention penalty. "Oh well," she said aloud, "I'll soon know whether Daddy Hanks is here for that reason or for something else."

When she entered the office, she had her answer. There with Mr. Drago sat Ms. Rhymer.

Mr. Hanks was a tall, lean man with sharp chiseled features. His hollow eyes, deeply set, and black hair gave him a striking resemblance to the portraits of Abraham Lincoln. Weeda remembered having met and talked with him when he came to sign the tuition-free entrance papers, an exemption made possible to needy Christian families through the combined donations of several civic and Christian organizations. At that time, they had discussed the school's provisions and his responsibilities.

Mr. Drago opened the discussion. "Mr. Hanks, please tell the ladies what you told me, your concerns about after-school discipline."

"I'm here 'cause the other day Hammie come home at dark and that's happened a coupla times lately, and I aim not for it to happen no more 'cause it ain't safe for a lad his age to be roamin' 'round on the back streets of Rushton right at dark. In this day and age with so much meanness, it ain't safe."

"I understand," said Mr. Drago, "that he had after-school detention as a disciplinary measure. Is that right?"

"That's what he told me, but the trouble he had with the teacher were not of his doin'. He said another chap later owned up to pullin' the prank, but Hammie got the punishment. That ain't right."

"Yes. I agree, and Ms. Rhymer says she has apologized."

"I did apologize to Hammie, and I'm sorry about it."

"I hear what you say. I ain't certain what he done ahead of that but both times he was dark gettin' home cause now the days are short and it gets dark early. I ain't here to cause trouble, but I won't have Hammie comin' home at dark. If he misses his ride, he has to walk that two miles through places that ain't safe for grown-ups, much less younguns. Me and Hammie, we understand each other. I don't worry and fret him about every little thing. I give him a lot of room to be Hammie. I don't believe in watching over younguns so they can't be younguns, but I do think they ought to be protected. I hold him to strict rules in big things but in little things me and his mama give him choices and some wiggle room. That way, he don't kick the big things that do matter 'cause he ain't mad and put out with us about things that don't make much difference."

Mr. Drago listened intently and chimed in, "Mr. Hanks, that's a commendable attitude. I wish more parents would deal with their children in that way. Your request is certainly reasonable. From now on, if the need to discipline Hammie arises, we'll find some means of solving the problem. In the event he is assigned to detention, we'll be responsible for getting him home safely. We were not aware of his transportation problem."

"I thank you. If Hammie gets into real trouble, I want to know about it, but I don't want to be bothered about nonsense. Just like I said before, me and my wife give Hammie room. I want to say again, we don't hound our younguns. We believe in doing what the Good Book says: 'Just leave them alone, and they'll come home, bringing their tails behind them.'"

The little conference broke up immediately.

* * *

At church Weeda was not in her usual place but had taken a seat on the other side of the sanctuary near the side entrance. While she and the lady on her right were exchanging greetings, she was aware that someone was taking a seat on her left, and when she turned around, she was face to face with Cody Houston and his wife. Weeda stiffened but hoped they didn't notice.

"Ms. McVey," said Anna, "we're glad to see you. Cody mentioned you yesterday." Then turning to her husband, "Cody, here's Ms. McVey."

"How are you, Ms. McVey? You don't usually sit in this section, do you?"

"No, I'm here so I can quickly slip out the side entrance at the end of the service."

"Oh my! Do people try to do school business at church, so you have to outrun them?"

"No, that's not it. For lunch I'm meeting a friend, Dr. Sanders. He's working at the hospital today, and his lunch time is limited, so I'll be in a hurry to get away."

"Dr. Sanders, eh? He's such a nice-looking man, and though I don't know him professionally, I have some friends who do, and they think he's wonderful. We see you two together frequently, and people are wondering, you know?"

"I'm not surprised. People do enjoy speculating. The service is just about to begin."

"But before it starts, let me say that Cody will probably be calling you next week. He wants to talk to you about Sonny. It's not urgent, I don't think." Weeda was glad the music was calling everybody to attention and hoped her lack of response went unnoticed.

While driving to Westwinds, she could think of nothing else. Something had to give. Macy wanted to discuss Sonny. Cody Houston wanted to discuss Sonny. She was the only one who had no desire to talk about Sonny, mainly because discussing Sonny would lead to discussing Cody, the father. She needed guidance and wisdom. "Grant it Father," was her prayer.

* * *

At Westwinds, the side porch was ideal for dining—the music soft, the temperature moderate, and the breeze gentle. Kyle thought Weeda looked stunning in her black and white suit accented by matching accessories. He liked the way she carried herself—a smooth gentle stride, more akin to waltzing than to walking. To those who didn't know, they might have suspected her to be a dance instructor, not a guidance counselor, though she definitely displayed the needed qualities of that profession as well. In conversation, she registered a person's every gesture, locking those soft brown eyes so intently that she seemed to be listening with her eyes as well as her ears. As they sat waiting, Kyle was thinking that for her, reading body language was like a second language, to her an innate ability which he had acquired only through extended effort and deliberate practice.

Since Kyle's lunchtime was limited, they selected from the menu the already prepared specialty of the day—grilled salmon with a citrus sauce. As the waiter retraced his steps back to the kitchen, Weeda started quizzing, a practice she tried to avoid outside the counseling office but one which she sometimes couldn't resist when it came to Kyle.

He was in some ways such an enigma. Since he had such a full medical practice, it puzzled her that he took on a self-imposed study of the Bible, not a study wherein he listened to others do expositions but a discipline given over to researching for himself. To her it was as though he wanted to reinvent the wheel. Why, she wondered, wasn't he content to learn from those who had already labored through the research? At that point, she gave voice to her thoughts.

"Kyle, you amaze me, poring over the Scriptures and resource materials as you do, using lexicons and all those reference materials. Do you have problems accepting the doctrines as taught by the church?"

"Weeda, we've been over all this before. I don't disagree with Dr. Crandall on what he preaches, but he, like many others, doesn't deal with some of the biblical topics which I find most interesting and consider essential."

"Such as?"

"The doctrine of Hell, the doctrine of demons, the doctrine of sin, the doctrine of the Second Coming. Besides, through others one gets to know about God; I want to know Him personally, and that comes through involvement in and through His Word."

"That's interesting. You say your digging will enable you to know Him better. I'm of the persuasion that if you've invited Him into your heart, He is there and makes Himself known."

"That's true, but there's a scripture, John 15:7, which reads, 'If ye abide in Me and My words abide in you, ask whatever you will and it shall be done unto you.' How do you meet that requirement?"

"You tell me."

"By studying and learning the Word for yourself, and you don't learn the Scriptures by listening to someone else expound and interpret. If you're going to know the Word to the degree that you can tap into the power inherent within it, then your love for and interest in it will very likely exceed that of the average church-going Christian. Then too, if this life is a prelude for the next, and I believe it is, then the most important thing a person can do in this life is prepare for the next. Agree?"

"Well yes, but how do you reconcile these convictions with the fact that you're a physician and have to prioritize your time according to the needs of others?"

"That's one of my dilemmas, and I'm wrestling for answers, but I'm convinced that when a person puts Christ first, God provides the solutions."

Kyle's beeper sounded, ending the conversation, but Weeda pondered on all these things as she drove slowly to her abode.

* * *

At Weeda's place later in the week, she and Kyle were slowly finishing their meal, a dinner of roast beef, potatoes, carrots, and a leafy salad. Suddenly, Kyle leaned forward and said, "You know, Weeda, we're so comfortable together, whether we're dining here at your place, eating out, visiting, attending church, or whatever. I think we should discuss just where this relationship is taking us, if anywhere. Yes?"

"You're asking me?"

"Nobody else here."

Shrugging her shoulders, she mumbled, "If I answer 'yes,' what in your thinking will be the focus of our dialogue?"

"Counselor McVey, can you tell me you've been so long at the conference table dealing with the intricacies of human relationships and you fail to pick up on such an implication? It was just a few days ago that I was admiring your intuitive nature. If, by chance, I was wrong in my assessment, your certification in counseling should be revoked."

"You're very blunt."

"That's part of being a diagnostician. You read the charts and tell it as you see it."

"You're saying that I'm not perceptive. How else does my chart read?"

"No, I'm really implying something else which, thus far, you have chosen to ignore. Each time I try to approach the subject of our relationship, you try to change the subject. Why?"

"I'm just not ready."

"That may be part of the truth but, my dear, it's not the whole truth, and you know it."

Obviously annoyed, she blurted out, "Dr. Sanders, since you're the diagnostician, you tell me. Suppose you answer your own question. What part of the truth is missing?"

"It's fear, Weeda, fear."

"Fear of what?"

"That's what you need to face. If you truly do not know what it is you fear, then you need to make an effort to find out."

"Find out what?"

"Why you're reluctant to discuss something as simple as a relationship. You've told me very little about your marriage. I know your husband was killed but little else. You talk freely about other people to whom you've been close—your brother and your mother, nothing about your father. Maybe you just don't like talking about the men in your life, so you've left me no choice. I have to speculate."

After a long silence, Weeda breathed out a heavy sigh. "So, Dr. Sanders, what conclusions have you reached through your speculations?" She was uncomfortable and it showed.

"To you my name is Kyle."

"And to you, I'm...uh! Are you aware that you started this conversation by disqualifying me as a counselor?"

"I know. I admit the sarcasm, so I'll permit you the same. But back to my assumptions. Either your love for Lanny was so deep and meaningful and the loss so traumatic that you can't deal with it, or your marriage was such a bad experience that you're ashamed to discuss it. Only you know."

She began to cry—big tears rolling down both cheeks.

"I'm sorry," said Kyle, "but it's time to talk about these things. What I do know about you, I fully appreciate. You have good taste in clothes and furnishings. Just look at this place. It's so well done, restful but colorful and coordinated. I know your moral and ethical standards, your taste in literature and music, the same standards that I value, but I know nothing of your emotional depth. You've built a wall around that part of your being and the gauge for measuring your feelings is hanging on your side of the wall. So after several months of seeing you, you have not allowed me to view that gauge."

"Please, Kyle, forgive me. I know I'm being unfair, but I can't. I just can't."

He realized she was hurting. "OK, I'll accept that for tonight. Let's do the dishes, and then I'll scoot. I have an appointment at seven in the morning." But while they were clearing the kitchen, Kyle couldn't resist pushing his point. "Weeda, if you can't discuss this fear with me then you need to find someone with whom you can discuss it."

"Are you suggesting therapy?"

"Possibly. When you're ready to talk about the future of our relationship, give me a call. Until then, I'll be spending what free time I have on my Bible studies. I still think you'd make a good sounding board, but that's up to you."

"You make it sound so complicated."

"You mean it's not? So if it's not complicated, then logically speaking, it must be simple, so what's the hold-up?"

"I promise to pray about it."

"That's a splendid idea. I hope you'll find a way to be more forthright with the Lord than you've been with me." With that, he hung up his dishtowel, gave her a quick side-to-side hug and left.

* * *

Weeda's buzzer sounded. "Yes?"

It was Mrs. Larson. "Two parental calls while you were at the library. Mrs. Turner had to cancel at the last minute—car trouble. Shortly after that Mr. Cody Houston called wanting to see you today if at all possible, saying he would be out of town next week, so I gave him Mrs. Turner's time slot."

With an edge in her voice she said, "Oh, uh, did you say Cody Houston?"

"Yes, any problem? He's probably on his way now. Mrs. Turner's appointment was for 2:15, and it's now 2:10. In fact, he's walking in the door now. Sonny's folder is lying on top in your priority basket."

"OK, uh, give me a few minutes. I'll buzz when I'm ready." Ready? She knew she wasn't ready to see Cody Houston, and couldn't get prepared if she had all day, so she bowed her head and quietly spoke to the Lord.

"Father God, I'm not ready to see this man; I don't want to hear what he has to say, particularly if it has anything to do with Sonny's adoption. Maybe I'm just fearful, so take away the fear. I'm hoping that he is here for some other concern and won't bring up the subject, but if he does, so be it. Help me to handle the situation and especially help me to handle myself. I thank You in advance for intervening in my behalf."

Calmness settled upon her but she still needed time to collect her thoughts. So she continued for a few more minutes to thank the Lord for His faithfulness and for answered prayer.

Cody Houston was a handsome middle-aged man in his early fifties. He was tall but not lanky, and his salt and pepper hair was always cut in a fashionable style. He was polished, forever the gentleman. His Tulane training served him well. After graduation, he traveled for a year before returning to Rushton to enter the lumber business with his father, Cody Cleveland Houston. The business and its sideline endeavors, all under the name of Houston Enterprises, had continued to flourish under Cody's management even after Papa Houston retired.

After working the business for a couple of years and several courtships, Cody started dating Anna Lassiter, a young lady from nearby Limestone whom he had met through his father when from time to time they took trips to that area to make lumber deals. Cody had considered Anna a good catch. She had so much to recommend her: good looks, good background, good fortune, and a good liberal arts degree from a small finishing school at Montevallo. She was very much a southern lady—always cordial, a bit naive and helpless when it was the befitting thing to do. Cody had been attracted to that feminine demeanor from the start, and after a few months of courtship, he married her.

In Limestone, the wedding was the social event of the season. Rushton's socialites, Houston's business associates, and members of the Protestant churches flocked out of town for the occasion. Many were envious of the couple—the young unmarried women of her and the eligible bachelors of him. "They were made for each other" was the buzz, and even they had considered themselves lucky to come together. All things progressed smoothly with no glitches in their relationship, that is, until they were told by several doctors that Anna would never be able to have children. The gloom descended. It was a disappointment they attempted to assuage through adoption.

In just a short time, Weeda gave Ms. Larson the signal that she was ready. He entered and sat down across the desk from her. After the usual polite greetings, Weeda was ready to get down to business.

"Mr. Houston, your wife mentioned at church you wanted to see me. It just so happened that I had a cancellation, so Ms. Larson was able to work you in today."

"I'm grateful. I'll be out of town for a week, so I wanted to talk with you before I left. Of course my reason for being here concerns Sonny."

"Yes, of course. In what way?"

"It's his attitude. He has changed these past few weeks. He has always been agreeable, well-mannered, accepting, but lately he's resentful, irritable, short-tempered, surly. I can't figure it out. To my knowledge, nothing at home has changed, so naturally, I'm looking elsewhere for explanations, and I'm wondering if something has happened here at school to account for such behavior?"

"I'm not aware of any changes here at school, but that doesn't rule out the possibility. Have you confronted him about these concerns?"

"No, not really. I've tried to treat his behavior lightly, hoping these negatives are somehow related to mood swings that will pass."

"Probably you need to make an appointment with him as you have with me and relay to him your observations. He might welcome the opportunity to open up."

"Yes, that's a logical approach, but I suppose I halfway dread what might come up."

"Meaning?"

"Uh, I, uh...Ms. McVey, you know that Sonny is an adopted child. I suppose for all adoptive parents there's that low-grade dread that some day the child will want to find out about his birth parents."

"Yes, I suppose that's a concern in many cases. Assuming the information is available, would it greatly disturb you and your wife if Sonny found out who his birth parents are and the reason why adoption was warranted?"

He looked down, and a lengthy silence followed. Finally, looking up, his eyes locked with Weeda's, and he replied, "Yes, definitely."

"Since that's the case, then for peace of mind you need to get to the bottom of Sonny's changed behavior. If it's a problem having to do with his adoption, you need to deal with it, but if it stems from some other source, then you still need to deal with that too. Finding a solution probably hinges on your opening up a discussion about his adoption."

"Oh, we've talked freely about his adoption in a general way since he was old enough to understand, but he has never been interested so far as we could detect about specifics."

"My advice to you is that you give him an opportunity to get specific if he has a need for that."

"Uh, unexpected advice. I'm not sure either of us is up to dealing with this."

"But, Mr. Houston, you're already dealing with it. You're under a dread and that in itself is dealing with the problem but not in a constructive way."

"Yes, I suppose you're right."

"If I perceive correctly, you're afraid Sonny's changed behavior stems from or is somehow related to his adoption, so if that's the case, you're both dealing with the same fear but in negative ways. Are you afraid of losing your son?" A response was slow in coming.

"Not legally, but I don't want to lose his affection and respect."

Weedy was hoping her racing thoughts were not registering in her voice and facial expressions. "Mr. Houston," she said, "these kinds of suspicions and uncertainties can wreck havoc in relationships. The sooner you face these doubts, the better. You might find that you're borrowing trouble since, I assume, the adoption was both moral and legal."

"Uh, uh, uh, yes, yes, yes." At this point he picked up his hat— an indication that he was ready to bring the discussion to a halt. "I shall certainly give your advice serious consideration. Please, I'm depending on your confidentiality in this matter."

"Of course. Have a good trip."

"Thank you, but with all these things on my mind, it won't be possible. I do appreciate your time." He uttered a hasty goodbye and departed.

Kyle had not had any contact with Weeda since the night he informed her he'd be busy doing other things until she was ready to discuss their relationship. That was two weeks ago. He was disappointed in not having heard from her but was positive he had done what needed to be done. If she refused to be honest and open about her past, it was better to face the truth: they didn't have a base for building a lasting relationship. He didn't need to be committed to someone whose deep-seated fears and hang-ups could wreak havoc later. But this rationale did little to erase her from his thoughts. He missed her company, the phone calls, and their Bible discussions.

Today he was at work, seeing patient after patient, but from time to time these thoughts kept flashing through his mind. On his return to the exam room after a restroom break, he met Ms. Kelly, his office manager in the hallway. "Dr. Sanders, a special delivery letter marked 'personal' was delivered a few minutes ago. I signed for it and placed it on your desk."

"Thank you, Jan. How many more patients before lunch break?"

"Two, plus the one in the exam room."

"Good, I'm hungry."

After finishing with the other two patients, he went to his office and on his desk was the letter Jan had mentioned. He had expected to see a legal-sized business envelope. Instead, there on personalized stationery in raised print was the name and return address of 'Weeda McVey.' He ripped it open, his mind racing ahead as to its content. It read:

Dear Kyle,

I've missed you and have given much thought to our last evening together. Amid my confusion, I've come to some conclusions: I don't think I'll go for therapy, at least not for now. I hope that after you have read this letter you'll still be inclined toward a continuation of our friendship. I'm reluctant to say relationship for fear that the following confession will lessen your desire to make it so.

Your insistence that I talk about my marriage is not unreasonable. In fact, it's essential. So if I'm in agreement with you, why have I remained silent? I can't answer that question specifically. I don't think I've ever been in complete denial, but perhaps in some aspects, I've come close. Perhaps I'm rationalizing, but I've conclud-

ed that writing these revelations will be easier than verbalizing them in person. Goodness knows! The writing is difficult enough.

I believe I told you how I met Lanny. We were both doing supervised research in the same school district in Tuscaloosa where we worked together on projects, seminars, etc. We clicked, so to speak, right away. By most people's standards, Lanny was considered a good catch. Therein lies much of my shame. Even while I was growing up, I considered myself a fairly good judge of human nature and character, but when it came to choosing a husband, I failed miserably in my assessment. As it turned out, Lanny was bisexual and his only definition of sex was of the oral variety, so Kyle, technically speaking, I am still a virgin. Now you know.

After a few weeks of trying to live with Lanny, I filed for an annulment. The proceedings had scarcely begun when his out-of-state ex-lover, upon learning of his marriage to me, came to Tuscaloosa where we both had taken permanent positions, and in an insane rage of jealousy murdered him. To say the least, I was traumatized. The memory is still painful, but God in His mercy has enabled me to carry on. I still wrestle with forgiveness, especially toward myself.

In my professional life, I like to think I have functioned well. In my personal life, I'm afraid I'm not meeting with much success. I'm still angry for allowing myself to be deceived. There are times when I feel contaminated, defiled, stained, tarnished. Prayer helps tremendously. When shame engulfs me, I try to find time to seek the Lord. He is faithful to provide a measure of cleansing, but at best the respite is temporary.

As a counselor, I know the wisdom of seeking professional help, so why have I not done so? I'm not sure. Maybe I've dreaded the pain of opening up. If these confessions should alter our friendship, I can understand. I would appreciate hearing from you. The next move is yours.

Weeda

He was stunned and reread the note several times to make sure he was getting the message she had intended. Seldom had he called Weeda at work, but he found himself punching in her school number, and Ms. Larson answered.

"Guidance office, Rushton Christian School."

"Yes, this is Dr. Kyle Sanders. I'd like to speak to Weeda McVey if she's available. It's a personal matter."

"Sure, I'll buzz her."

After a moment, Weeda came on the line.

"Weeda, this is Kyle. I just read your letter. What are you doing tonight?"

She was overcome; she couldn't get her speech mechanisms coordinated with her thoughts. "Kyle, I'm, uh, this is fourth Thursday and I have that little supper club to attend, the one with the school's female faculty members."

"Could you cut out for once?"

"I suppose I could, but I'll have to make arrangements to provide the beverages as I promised. What do you have in mind?"

"Just getting together in a place where we can talk—your place or mine."

"My place is fine, but I'll be busy getting drinks and ice delivered at the meeting place, so there won't be much to eat from my kitchen."

"That's no problem. The Big Tree has excellent carryouts; I'll bring dinner. What would you like?"

"Let me think. Whatever will be fine. Why don't you select for me?"

"OK, I'll see you. I should be there around seven."

* * *

A few hours later inside Weeda's kitchen, Kyle put the food cartons on the dining table and turned toward Weeda, who had rushed to the stove to turn down the burner under the whistling teakettle. When she turned back around, they stood only a few strides apart in an awkward, tense moment. Kyle moved toward her and taking her in his arms whispered, "Weeda, you should have unloaded sooner. What a burden you've been carrying."

"I was afraid to risk your finding out how stupid I had been."

"Stupid?"

"To allow myself to fall into such a predicament."

"We'll talk about that later. What gave you the idea I wouldn't understand?"

"Well, you always come across as having it all together. I was embarrassed..." Whatever she was trying to say never became audible. He had her mouth covered with kisses, kisses portraying the message that she was accepted in spite of her past.

When he finally did speak, his words tied back into her last statement: "Because you think I have it all together and you don't, you hide behind a wall, eh?"

"Maybe so, I don't know. I suppose pride has played a part."

All the time Kyle was maneuvering her toward the sofa in the den. There he cradled her head on his shoulder saying, "Now cry your heart out; that's partly what you need," and she did just that. No uttered words, just sobbing sounds coming from a broken heart and a wounded spirit. Finally, the sobbing subsided, replaced by long sighs that smacked of relief and resignation. Then came a question.

"Kyle, you must be starved. Your dinner has gotten cold."

"Never mind. In making a selection, I suspected that once I was here, the dining would be delayed, so I brought something that could be reheated—a beef stew and some of Sammy's scrumptious biscuits. A few whirls in the microwave will to it."

They ate slowly, still coming down from the emotional throes of the kiss and, for Weeda, the relief that she had been totally accepted. The hedges around the core of her being had been greatly affected by that revealing acceptance. Satisfying the appetite was not really important just now. Other irons in the fire deserved her attention. They talked long into the night. Finally, Kyle looked at his watch and said, "Weeda, I've been studying more and more about how some Christians are dealing with their emotional and spiritual hang-ups, and I'd like to share these findings with you—a couple of books I'd like you to read, but enough of that for tonight. We both need to get to bed. I have an early appointment with a man who needs both physical and spiritual help, so I'm going to say goodnight." With a light little peck to her cheek, he quickly departed.

At midnight, Weeda was in bed mulling over Kyle's reaction to her confession when the telephone rang.

"Hello?"

"Ms. McVey, this is Sonny Houston."

"Yes, Sonny, I recognize your voice, but you sound..."

"Ms. McVey," his voice trembling, "I need you to pray for me."

Startled out of her drowsy lull, she blurted out, "Where are you?"

"I can't say, but I'm calling to ask you to pray for me."

"Of course! But I need to know more, so I'll know how to pray. Are you ill, in danger, or what?"

"I'm in a tight spot. Just pray I'll get out and nobody will know. Please keep this call secret. Gotta hang up. Bye."

She hung up and sat on the side of the bed in a daze. After a lapse of several minutes, she knelt down by the bed and prayed. "Dear Lord, Sonny is one of Your children. I come to the Throne of Grace in his behalf and bring his predicament with me. I don't know what the trouble is, but You do, for nothing is hidden from Your eyes. He says he is in a tight spot and is seeking release. I am grateful that he knows You and understands Your power to deliver in times of need. This knowledge he has of You has prompted him to seek Your help by requesting prayer. Please honor this faith he places in You and add my faith to his and let us have a solution. Your Word assures us that with You nothing is impossible, so Father, in the Name of Jesus I ask You to orchestrate in his behalf. If this trouble is of his own making, then may he learn a lesson from this mistake, but do have mercy and bring him out a wiser and more mature young man. If he is the victim of someone else's misdeeds, then fight for him as only You can do and give him victory. And Lord, I ask for wisdom in dealing further with this concern. You have promised that if we ask for wisdom, You will give liberally and upbraid us not. I ask these things in confidence, knowing that You are always faithful in answering prayer. Amen."

The next morning, immediately upon entering the office, Weeda instructed Ms. Larson to send her the absentee list as soon as it was distributed. Though she didn't make it known, she was anxious to know whether or not Sonny was in school. If so, she'd have a measure of relief; otherwise she'd be concerned about the why of his absence and the whereabouts of his person. In the event of his absence, should she inquire and to whom? Were the Houstons aware of last night's tight spot? To say the least, she was in a quandary and very much distracted from other concerns of the day.

There were several students in the waiting area who needed advice about scholarship applications. Though she had provided filled-out sample forms to all seniors, some students still needed help. She briefly counseled with each of those waiting and answered their questions. After finishing with them, she glanced at the clock and realized first period was almost over. Where was the absentee list? At that moment, the intercom clicked on. It was the secretary announcing that the computer was down and the absentee lists would be delayed.

"Oh my!" she said half-aloud, "I can't wait to know. Where is Houston first period?" Quickly she thumbed through her Rolodex roster. "Here he is: Houston, Rajah Lee (Sonny), First Period, U. S. Government, Room 114. Uh huh," she thought, "in three minutes classes will change."

Grabbing a working clipboard, she walked down the corridor toward the Government classroom and took a stand just outside 114 so she'd be able to identify the students as they exited. She was trying to fake absorption with the clipboard when the bell rang. Her wait was short and her answer immediate. The third person out the door was Sonny Houston. She looked directly at him, expecting him to acknowledge her, but after glancing in her direction, he quickly diverted his eyes, dropped his head, and walked briskly down the hall. She was greatly relieved that he was in school but completely baffled by his evasive behavior.

Weeda had finished her after-school phone calls and was making ready for a quick exit home when a knock on the door summoned her to answer. To her amazement there stood Macy looking distraught and a bit disheveled.

"Macy, what brings you here at this time of the day?"

"I'm sorry, Ms. McVey, I just had to talk to you. I'm so upset."

"Yes, that's evident." Without asking, Weeda knew Sonny was the reason for Macy's distress, but she asked anyway. "What's this all about?"

"Ms. McVey, it's Sonny."

Dreading an answer but anxious to know, she responded. "What about Sonny?"

"I can't prove it, but I believe he's doing drugs."

"Oh no, what makes you suspect that?"

"It's his behavior and his excuses. He's not honest with me about where he goes and what he does. He's not himself, and he worries, worries, worries."

A recall of Sonny's adoption concerns prompted Weeda to counter with, "But Macy, the fact that he worries is not necessarily a sign of drug use, is it?"

"But that's not all. He's connecting to some of the kids at Woodland High, and they're not the right connections."

"In what way is he connecting?"

"He's hanging out with some of the boys and nobody knows where they go."

"Is he still attending the youth sessions at the church?"

"Not regularly, and when he does go, he seems to be miserable and not himself."

"Meaning what?"

"He's distracted, and when we're together, we're not in sync. He's preoccupied. He doesn't listen. I have to repeat myself in order to register with him."

Weeda yearned to reject what she was hearing but found it impossible, remembering that late-night prayer request and his avoidance of her since that time. She wished she were not bound by confidentiality concerning his family problems and prayer request. Things needed to come to light regardless of the immediate consequences. "Have you shared these concerns with your parents?"

"Oh no. If they knew, they wouldn't want me to see him anymore. Ms. McVey, why is life so complicated for young folks?"

"That's a full-sweeping question, not only for the young but for people of all ages. Having said that, I agree that young people today are up against situations that at best are confusing and at worst horrendous and sometimes devastating. Do you think the youth minister has noticed these changes in Sonny?"

"Probably not, not this one. He's so different from the director before. He taught the Bible but this one doesn't, and the focus has changed."

"In what way?"

"Well, it's all about 'how-to,' and I'm finding that a 'how-to' for one person is not necessarily the 'how-to' for someone else."

"Well said, Macy. Are these session Bible centered?"

"Partly, I suppose. I don't know exactly what to say about them."

"What's the focus—the topic—of the meetings now?"

"We're working on becoming socially secure."

"That sounds like a concern most young people would consider important."

"I suppose so, but the discussions don't have substance or Scripture study. They don't get down to the nitty-gritty—that most teenagers are unhappy. Don't you agree?"

"Oh, I don't know. I haven't thought precisely about numbers and percentages, but here at school I would hope the number of really unhappy students is few in number."

"Let me assure you that the number is not small. Many of those who appear to be happy are faking it. Most of my friends are Christians, for which I'm grateful, but they're not happy Christians, much less happy people."

"Are you including yourself?"

"Yes, I am. I was doing all right until recently. This thing with Sonny is pulling me down."

"I can see that, but apart from this recent disappointment, you are established in your faith, aren't you?"

"I hope I am, but this kind of experience does raise questions that seem to have no answers."

"What do you think this school could do to help youth to find answers?"

"I'm not savvy enough to answer that, but sometimes I do think that both the church and the schools are falling down on the job. Seems the schools should teach the basics—study skills, occupation-al skills, and all those things, and the church should minister and provide the answers for our spiritual needs so we can stay glued together regardless of circumstances. Am I off key?"

"I can't say you are. In fact, I'm amazed at your insight and the way you have separated the roles of the school and that of the church. How do you think the church programs might be improved?"

"By teaching the fundamentals necessary to live a victorious Christian life: the necessity of prayer and how to pray, how to recog-nize temptations and resist them, the necessity of forgiveness. I just wish they'd take a different approach."

"Very good suggestions. You took the required freshman and sophomore Bible courses here. Were they helpful?"

"Yes, they were, but I think Bible should be required all four years. I haven't had any organized instruction since the tenth grade except in Sunday school, and those lessons have no depth. We pret-ty much deal with a different topic every Sunday. Why don't you start a Bible study for those who would be interested?"

"You mean here?"

"Maybe, but if not here then outside the school."

"Macy, I'm flattered you'd make that suggestion. I don't feel I'm qualified to teach Bible, but I am impressed that you see the need for such a study. Why don't we make your suggestion a matter of prayer, asking God to open doors if that's His will, to send someone to lead the study?"

"I'll certainly agree to that, and will you pray for Sonny? I don't want our friendship to end." After that request, she realized she had to hurry for a dental appointment and said so. She departed quick-ly.

That night on the phone Weeda shared with Kyle a part of her earlier conversation with Macy. He too was amazed at her viewpoints, especially that she differentiated the role of the school from that of the church.

"I must say," said Kyle, "in this situation the counselee seems to have become the counselor—a role reversal."

"To say the least! And when such reversals occur, I try to benefit."

"By all means. I sometimes have similar experiences with my patients. You'll follow up on this right away, I presume?"

"Sure. She says there is a great need for a Bible study, one organized and taught apart from either the school or the church. And Kyle, I was astounded at the topics she thought should be emphasized. I jotted them down."

"Such as?"

"Would you believe? Learning to pray with faith and power; leading people to Christ; avoiding pitfalls and resisting temptations; consequences of sinning."

"Wow! That kid's right on!"

"It's so refreshing to find a young person with such enthusiasm for the things of God. We talked again by phone, after I came home, and I laughingly told her she should consider a college major in sociology with a specialty in societal pathology."

"Good counseling, I'd say. Tell me her name again."

"Macy. Macy Bryant."

"Macy Bryant? Umm, I think I know her parents—patients of mine. Herbert and Leslie Bryant. It's not surprising she's precocious."

"She and I have agreed to pray about the Bible study, and if God opens the door, we'll need a teacher, a leader."

"Why don't you volunteer?"

"Strange you should say that. Macy suggested the same thing."

"Sounds like a confirmation to me."

"Not so fast, Kyle. You know I don't know the Bible that well."

"One way to learn is to teach."

"So they say, but I can't see myself in that role. I'm not the scholar you are."

"That's your opinion. I'm not scholar, but I am interested in what God has revealed and am willing to spend some time to find out."

"Doesn't that partially define a scholar?"

"Maybe, to a degree. Scholars usually want to share through teaching or writing, publishing papers. I don't have that urge."

"Could you be persuaded in that direction?"

"With my work load? Only if I felt it was a directive from the Lord."

"Well, as I said, Macy and I have agreed to make the study a matter of prayer, so you might receive such a directive."

"And Weeda, my dear, while you're praying, you might want to keep in mind the old adage that you shouldn't present to God a problem unless you're willing to be used in the solution of it. You might be just the one who gets the teaching directive."

"Kyle, you always have a topper for everything. I'm sleepy, so do you mind if we finish this discussion at another time?"

"Not at all, but before we hang up, I want to remind you that I have that book on prayer counseling that I mentioned. I'll get it to you right away."

"Good. Right now I'm a candidate for both prayer and counseling, separately or combined."

"Aren't we all? Sweet dreams."

After she hung up, she quietly whispered, "Dear Lord, I have too many pressing irons in the fire. I need to read Kyle's book. I need, so Kyle thinks, to get counseling for myself, and first and foremost, I need to alert the Houstons that Sonny's grades are spiraling downward. Than You, Lord, that I can use his failing grades as a reason to call them in for a conference. Lord, involve Yourself in Sonny's life and bring Your spirit to bear on his tormenting situation. I know Sonny loves You, but he's caught up in a horrible dilemma. Remaining silent has put him in reverse. He's losing out, but if he speaks up, he fears for his father's reputation and the possible breakup of the home. I now think he should tell his parents what he found out and trust You to determine what chips fall where. If he can get this adoption secret off his shoulders, surely with Your help his other problems can be resolved. Frankly Lord, I think I overestimated Sonny's emotional strength. I had thought he could handle these pressures, but I was wrong. I'm trusting You to lead me so I can better advise. Tonight I'm joining Macy in asking, 'Why is life sometimes so difficult?' Will I hurt less after I have been through prayer counseling? And Lord, while I have Your ear, I want to mention the Bible study. If such an effort can serve Your purposes for the young people in Rushton, then give a Godly green light to the leaders of your choice. Lay it on their hearts to take the initiative for getting

organized. Open the doors. And Lord, orchestrate as only You can
do, the means by which I can assist the Houstons and their son.
Thank You for hearing and answering prayer. Amen."

* * *

Kyle was preparing his dinner and wishing he could talk to
Weeda, so he rang her number.

"Hello?"

"Hi Weeda, have you eaten?"

"No, but I'm hungry."

"Good, I'll put two steaks on the grill. Come on over."

"Are you serious? I've just shampooed my hair."

"Don't you blow dry?"

"Well, yes, but...."

"Good. We'll eat as soon as you get here."

Weeda sat watching from the bar stool as Kyle put the finishing
touches on the meal: grilled T-bones, steamed buttered potatoes, a
medley of raw fresh veggies, and garlic bread, lightly toasted. She
was impressed and said so. "Kyle, when, where, and how did you
arrange to become so domestic?"

"Domestic? Is that what you call it? I always thought of it as sur-
vival tactics."

"Whatever the label, how did you get so good at it?"

"If I wanted to eat well, or eat at all, I had to either eat out, which
gets monotonous, or learn to shift for myself, so in the shifting
process, I learned a few tricks and procedures: how to cook, how to
shop, and some other lesser skills to facilitate my simple lifestyle."

"And don't leave out the housekeeping. Your place is always neat
and orderly."

"Gee, thanks but I can't take all the credit for that. I've been for-
tunate to have good cleaning ladies. The one I have now is fairly
new."

"Is that Evanne you've told me about?"

"Right. She comes on Tuesdays and Fridays. She's a steady, reli-
able worker but short, very short on imagination—no sense of
humor. Everything to her is literal and set in concrete."

"You've mentioned that before. Any recent incidents or examples?"

"Glad you asked. I didn't want to forget to tell you. When I hired
her, I knew she was a friend of Lessie's, the lady who preceded her.

So I wanted her to understand why I let her friend go—that I didn't hire and fire without reasons. I explained that Lessie had serious health problems, diabetes coupled with very high blood pressure and shouldn't be here working alone, that I was afraid I might come home and find her in a coma. She seemed to accept my reasoning, and I thought no more about it. Well, last Tuesday during my mid-day break, I came home to munch on some leftovers. When I walked into the den, there stood Evanne with her hands on her hips, a stance one couldn't ignore, though at first I tried. Then when she continued to hold such a pose, I couldn't refrain, so I asked, 'Evanne, is something wrong? Why are you just standing there'? To which she replied, 'Well, Sir Doctor,' she always calls me that, 'I always does this when you drives up; you jess ain't noticed afore today. You see, I ain't forgot what you told me 'bout my friend Lessie, why you let her go. I sho don't wanna lose this here job, so ever time you drives up, no matter where I is, I goes and stands in the middle of the room fer a coupla minutes. I can't fergit you let her go 'cause you wuz 'fraid you'd come home and find her in a corner.'"

Weeda cracked up saying, "What did you do at that point?"

"I tried as best I could to ease her fears. Again, she appeared to understand, but who knows what might turn up next. There's absolutely no foolishness in her, but sometimes the byproduct of her behavior becomes the most foolish of all foolishness."

They were both hungry and ate heartily. Toward the end of the meal, Weeda sensed from Kyle's demeanor that something was on his mind—that the small talk was coming to a close. She had already begun bracing herself for whatever. Then it came.

"How are you doing? That is, concerning the guilt and shame which besets you from time to time?"

So that was it. "Oh, I'm coming along. I stay so busy I don't have time to think about myself."

"Yeah, work's a good opiate. I don't mean that altogether negatively. It really is, but one can't work all the time. Work brings fatigue and fatigue calls for rest. So when you reach that point and do rest, what are your feelings?"

"Kyle, I must say I have noticed some difference since I unloaded on you that night."

"Good. I hope you'll consider the prayer counseling I mentioned to you."

"I remember, but I'm at a loss! I haven't gotten around to the book you gave me, and I do pray, if that's what you mean. I just never heard of prayer counseling in any of my studies."

"I'm sure you're right about that. It's not a part of the educational curriculum. I'm talking about counseling sessions wherein a counselee and a confessor bring the counselee's hurts and sins before the Lord for cleansing, for forgiveness, and possibly for the healing of a broken heart and a wounded spirit."

"I know people who pray for those things in their own way but not in counseling sessions. No, I can't exactly relate to that concept. Never heard of it, but I can tell you're dying to inform me."

"Your perception is keen tonight. Let me start by saying that I have not only studied these procedures but I've actually had personal experience with them. I myself have benefited from such help, and I have assisted others in finding release from emotional and spiritual bondage. It's scriptural."

"In what way?"

"James 5:14-15." He opened the top drawer of the sideboard and pulled out a New Testament and turning to that particular passage, he handed it over and said, "There, read it for yourself." She read it and then responded.

"Yes, but this says you're to call for the elders of the church. You're not an elder."

"True, my dear, but tie this command in with other similar passages and you have one of God's assignments to all believers. Also His remedy for healing a plethora of ills and confusions of the Christian family."

"Well, if it works and is so effective, why don't the churches promote it?"

"A few do, but many don't for the same reason they fail to emphasize other biblical mandates. I try not to fault them for what they don't do, though I wish they'd do more. Criticism seldom brings about change. But just because they, and that's the majority of Christians, don't attach importance to these available blessings is no reason why I should ignore them. A person's salvation and relationship to God is personal, not corporate. So I'm personally responsible for what I believe and practice. Agree?"

"Yes. I mean, I don't know. You amaze me. How and where did you come to know about this prayer counseling?"

"I'll get to that as we go along. It's not too different in some ways from the counseling you do. You use principles of psychology, which have merit as far as they go, but in many cases they don't go far enough, and besides the emphasis is often misdirected. The aim of psychology is to restore clients to functional levels, which is commendable. Prayer counseling goes further. Its aim is to subdue and tame man's sinful nature by bringing it to death at the Cross. As I said, restoring a person so he can function is beneficial, but for purposes of wholeness, it is incomplete.

"Also, psychology holds to the theory that life's experiences determine the who and what of a person—that people are who they are because of what they've experienced. Much of that theory is true, but it's not the whole truth. Such a view discounts sin, the power of sin, and the truth about man's sinful nature, which as you know, we all inherited from the first man to sin. Sins need to be forgiven, and that can be had for the asking, but the subduing requires participation, and sometimes, hard work. The rebirth can come instantly by recognizing Jesus as Lord and Savior, but deliverance often requires reaching back into a person's formative years to a time or situation where the person either committed sinful deeds or was sinned against. Sexual abuse, for example. Many redeemed Christians are in bondage because they were sexually abused as children and their scars have never been removed. These adults are hampered in their personalities and spirits by such scarring. A person's love life can be drastically affected. For example, some women's ability to trust men is completely fractured. The success of these sessions hinges on the client's willingness to confess his sins and to forgive those who have sinned against him or her. The Apostle Paul wrestled with these very things. Read the sixth and seventh chapters of Romans."

"Are you suggesting I avail myself of this kind of help?"

"Yes, I am, but not with me. It's prudent to seek help from someone who is not related to the client in any way—a person who is able to be objective and can lay the axe to the root of the tree, so to speak, a person who can call a spade a space, call sin what it is: sin. Sometimes, it's like having surgery. As you know, one of the effective ways to cure cancer is to cut it out, and so it is with some of man's sinful nature—excise it using the power of the Cross and the blood of Jesus. Prayer counseling avoids all the euphemisms: maladjustments, deviations, aberrations, and the like. For one who has committed sin, the remedy is confessing the sin and receiving forgiveness. For those who have been sinned against, the remedy is extending forgiveness toward the person or persons who have violated them. Receiving and extending forgiveness provides the divine medicine so often needed to heal a multiplicity of problems that plague God's children."

"Whew, my head's spinning! I can't take it all in."

"You don't have to be hasty. Try reading and digesting the book at your own pace."

"Even if I should get sold on the idea, I wouldn't know where to start. I don't know anybody, but I assume you do."

"Yes, we'll discuss those things further down the line." He saw her to her car, gave her a quick hug, reminding her to drive carefully and give him a ring as soon as she reached home.

She drove home slowly, pondering those things Kyle had thrown at her and wondering if she should listen further to his suggestions. Having minored in psychology, she valued much of what she had been taught because she had seen the application thereof produce good results. True, some and perhaps many secular counselors were humanistic in their beliefs and practices. Christians just needed to be circumspect and prudent in choosing professional help of any kind whether it be for emotional, physical, financial, or legal reasons. Perhaps when she phoned Kyle tonight she just might argue these points, but then she didn't have much of a basis for argument since he had not discounted psychology altogether. He had merely emphasized the additional good that came through prayer counseling. On second thought, perhaps she'd better not bring up the subject again tonight. And she might be wise to read the book he recommended.

She knew she needed help from somewhere. There were times when her fears clouded her judgment and affected her counseling work. Sometimes the students' problems disturbed the recesses of her memory, causing painful vibrations that rendered her almost dysfunctional or so it seemed. She wanted to believe that others had never noticed, but there was Kyle who was aware of her problem, and he was the one who mattered most, the one she had hoped would never notice. She knew her professional strengths but she also recognized her shortcomings. Kyle was trying to be helpful, but she resented the fact that he was able to read her like an open book. Such perception on his part eliminated the element of intrigue, so essential in her thinking for the development of romance. "My!" she said aloud. "My thoughts are racing out of bounds."

Shortly after reaching home, she phoned Kyle as she had promised but mentioned nothing of her misgivings. She went to bed but sleep didn't come. Her body yearned to shut down but her mind wouldn't cooperate. She dreaded going to school in the morning. How she wished the Houston problem could be resolved.

She had not heard from Sonny since the night he called for prayer. Why had he not followed up with her after that? She had a foreboding feeling that Macy's fears were justified. How could the boy's turmoil subside when he was holding information which if known could wreck the Houston marriage? "Oh Lord," she prayed, "Do You still speak through dreams? I could surely use some divine guidance."

* * *

It was Saturday morning, and Kyle was up before dawn. His fishing gear was ready, and he was filling his cooler with snacks and drinks when the phone rang. He just let it ring. Dr. Chestnut was on call for the group, so he could handle whatever. When it continued ringing, he took a peek at the ID. It was Weeda. Why would she be calling at this hour?

"Hi Weeda," he said with anxiety in his voice. "Are you all right?"

"Yes and no."

"What do you mean?"

"Kyle, I knew you'd be leaving early, so I just had to tell you that I haven't even been to bed. I've been so absorbed in that book you wanted me to read that I could not put it down. Though I've been impressed enough to read all night, there are parts of it that have me in a dither."

"I'm listening. Be specific. What is it you can't receive?"

"Well, for one thing, the counselors seem to have no empathy, no understanding, They are so blunt, but they report good results."

"Exactly, and the good comes directly from the Lord Jesus working through the power of the Holy Spirit. These direct methods are what I call 'laying the axe to the root of the tree.' The counselors are His instruments."

"Well, it has me stirred up."

"That's understandable. You'd probably be wise to deal with your feeling while you are stirred up or at least talk through some things. I can go fishing another time if you want to talk."

"But you said you wouldn't be the one to take me through these prayers since we're..."

"Since we're what?"

"Kyle, don't taunt me. You're the one who said I should be counseled by someone who could be completely candid and objective."

"I wasn't suggesting you spill over to me. I'm merely thinking of discussing parts of the book which you feel need clarification. Shall I fish today or talk with you?"

"Go fishing. You need a break, and if you're not too tired, we can talk tonight or tomorrow."

"I have to run. Gotta pick up my buddy in about ten minutes. I'll give you a call when I get home."

* * *

That evening around nine Kyle called Weeda.

"Hi Kyle. How was fishing?"

"Great! We dragged them in early on, then they quit biting, but near sundown they started biting, and we dragged them in again. It was fun."

"What did you do with your catch?"

"Threw most of them back but saved some for Evanne. She and her family like those bream and small bass. She'll refrigerate a few bream and fry them for me next Tuesday when she comes to clean."

"Kyle, you know you shouldn't eat fried foods."

"How could I forget when you continue to remind me even though I continue to tell you that if I can't have my bream fried, then give me something else to eat? Bream are bream only if they're fried brown and crispy. Did you finish the book?"

"Yes, I did and then slept until about two and did my grocery shopping this afternoon. I tried to stay busy to keep my mind off the book. Every time I think about going through such a counseling process, I get panicky."

"You know who's responsible for those fears, don't you?"

"Off hand, I'd say I am, but the book lays the blame on the enemy who does every imaginable thing to prevent Christians from going through these experiences, so I'm trying to shift the blame on the Evil One. Am I on target?"

"Of course. The devil pressures us Christians with secondary fears to prevent our seeking freedom from the primary ones."

"Wow! I'll have to ponder that one, or have you clarify it for me later. What else do you think he might try?"

"Who knows, but we'll get busy and through prayer cancel out his nefarious designs. I need some sleep, but I'll pray for you before

I go to bed. I think I'll sleep in tomorrow. Why don't you meet me for lunch after church?"

"OK. Where? At Westwinds?"

"Sounds good to me. About 12:30."

* * *

It was 12:30, and Kyle, after claiming his reservations at Westwinds, waited in the lobby, watching the people as they filed in for the restaurant's good food and service. With nothing particular on his mind, he became keenly observant of what these after-church diners were wearing, especially the women. For the most part, those below fifty were clad in tight-fitting tubes that were supposed to pass for dresses. In his mind, the word "dress" connoted a style individualized for the purpose of enhancing. There was nothing individual and very little enhancing about these tubes. They had almost all things in common. They were tight, they were clingy, and they were mini. The only variations lay in the choice of color and the width of the shoulder straps. Just recently, he had heard his mother refer to them as apparel, which should be worn as underwear and kept in a drawer with the other lingerie. Sameness, sameness, and that went as well for the hairstyles or lack thereof. He wondered if some of the girls had misplaced their combs and upon arising that morning had not known where to find them. "Well," he said half-aloud, "I'll have some visual relief when Weeda arrives." And he did.

She was wearing a lovely jacket dress—a lavender knitted crepe. The hemline fell just below the knee, the right length for her build and height. He liked the way she dressed and comported herself, but to him it was evident that some aspects of her personality were misdirected by an inordinate amount of guilt and fear. Hopefully, with God's interventions, those negatives could be eliminated.

After they were seated, Weeda apologized. "Sorry I've kept you waiting. Several people joined the church today and that extended the after-service time."

"No problem! That kind of good news is worth waiting for. Besides, watching the people turned out to be entertaining. Would you believe I was caught up in what they were wearing? For days, all I see are exam gowns and hospital shirts. Wish I could say I was favorably impressed with what I observed today."

"Keep talking. I'm interested in what you think."

"Well, there seems to be a universal urge to expose as much flesh as is allowable, and goodness knows that's just about everything. I suppose the half-nudes believe that exposed flesh attracts, but I think not. To that point, I'm reminded of a verse by Emily Dickinson which, if I remember, goes something like this: 'The thought beneath so light a film/ Is more distinctly seen/ As laces just reveal the surge/ And mists the Apennines.'"

"Oh Kyle, you're so literate. I remember Emily Dickinson as an American poet, but I can't quote a thing she wrote. However, I do get the meaning, I think."

"Sure you do: That which is covered or slightly veiled is often more intriguing, especially from a sexual standpoint, than that which is exposed, mainly because the imagination is brought to play in the former but not the latter."

The waiter arrived and took their orders for grilled chicken breasts, saffron rice, and steamed green vegetables. Quickly, they discarded all thoughts of small talk and got down to the nitty-gritty of the book and Weeda's related concerns.

"Weeda, I've been praying that God will give you peace about reaching out for help."

"Thank you. I can feel the effects of your prayers, but I still don't understand why, if God is all powerful as I believe Him to be, why He can't just answer my simple requests by taking away whatever needs to be eliminated from my life."

"Many times, He does just that, but sometimes there are problems and areas of people's lives when, for reasons we don't always understand, He remains seemingly, and I emphasize seemingly, passive—situations that do not respond to ordinary prayer, ordinary discipline, and ordinary willpower. Sometimes it takes specific confessions accompanied by spiritual warfare to break such evil strongholds. I don't understand it all, but I know the reality of it, just as I don't understand the rebirth, but I know the reality of it. There are times when God steps into a situation and rights every wrong, but there are other times when He expects the Christian to use the weapons of warfare as relayed to us by Paul in Ephesians. Jesus Himself gave us several examples. He didn't ask the Father to set the Epileptic free. He issued the command and then chided the disciples for their failure to do so. Paul did a similar thing with the girl who was afflicted with a spirit of divination. He didn't pray. He commanded. Christians have spiritual power, but because they are not aware of it, that power lies dormant."

"Why then don't Christians take authority over the wrongs in the schools for instance and make things right?"

"Weeda, do you realize what a simplistic remedy you are trying to apply to a very complicated problem? Think about the ratio of believers to nonbelievers. The unsaved and unjust people of the world carry a power too, though they may not know it. Their powers in our social order can counter the powers of the saved. People seem to forget when assessing the ills of society that the social order belongs to Satan. God owns the earth, the real estate, but until Christ returns, the social order will continue to be Satan's realm, and you and I will have to function within these confines, but that doesn't preclude our seeking a measure of freedom within these confines. Here's our food."

While they were eating, Weeda kept up her questioning. "I know you must be right, but I've always considered the blessings of God to be free for the asking."

"Many are. Through faith we gain eternal life, but victory over such things as generational bondage, curses, and many emotional hang-ups come only as a result of spiritual warfare. Paul teaches this truth in Ephesians, Chapter Six. So many Christians have little or no knowledge about the invisible yet real war going on between God and Satan."

"But Jesus has already won the victory."

"True—the decisive battle, but the war continues. Satan and his emissaries continue the fight mainly through deceptions. Show me a Christian walking by faith who doesn't have to fight. Do you know one?"

"I'd never thought along those lines until I read the book. It's hard for me to grasp it all."

"At the risk of sounding didactic and boring, let me back up. As the psalmist wrote: 'The earth is the Lord's and the fullness thereof'—the planet, the real estate that is—but as I've already said, the social order, since the day of Adam's fall, has been Satan's domain. That was God's reason for sending the Second Person of the Trinity to earth—to continue the liberating and reclaiming procedure he had begun through Noah and then continued through Abram. Because God's original contract concerning the earth was made with a man, it is imperative that any negotiations related to the management of it be carried out through a man—not an angel or any other order of being. The main contractors are referred to as the First Adam and the Second Adam. Since man is the voice for the carrying out of earthly business, both God and Satan use him to carry out their purposes. Though God can and sometimes does overrule and override by using ungodly people, for the most part, he uses committed Christians to promote his plan of redemption just as Satan uses non-Christians to promote his planned program for one day taking over the world through an anti-Christ. So sad to say, Satan is supported in his ambitions through masses of unbelieving people and is looking for a man who will one day personify him in the same way that Jesus stood up for God the Father at Cavalry by carrying out His commission. When Satan finds and indwells such a man, whom he is possibly already grooming, he will use him to control the earth for a period of time, but that control will be brought to an end by Christ at the Battle of Armageddon." Kyle pushed his empty plate aside saying, "I didn't mean to lecture."

"No problem. I'm impressed, though I can't put it all together at once. Please continue."

"Well, back to your question of asking and receiving. God answers prayer, as you well know, but as I've already stated, there are times when believers must stand up and remind the enemy that the decisive battle has been won and that God's will takes precedence over the will of the enemy. Only then in the Name of Jesus do the evil forces concede and withdraw their influence and power. That is the premise on which successful Christian counseling is based."

"The book brings out some of these concepts, but it helps to hear you summarize them. I was taken with the author's ideas about generational bondages."

"Yeah, in my practice I see evidence of such carryovers. Because of the sinful practices of ancestors, much pain and suffering have been passed down from generation to generation. Family feuding, divorce, immorality, addictions, and alcoholism are some of the generational curses that can be broken by a Christian who knows how to operate strategically in spiritual warfare. There is such a wealth of knowledge that Christians can come into if they will only believe the Bible and submit to the teachings and leading of the Holy Spirit."

"Apparently, you have come into much of that knowledge, but me, I'm about as smart as Howdy Doody when it come to spiritual know-how."

"Now, now, you're too hard on yourself. All you need is your appetite whetted. I have just begun to nibble, but I hope to keep at it until, as Paul said, I've been weaned from milk and can digest solid food. The counseling sessions will likely bring about some of the whetting you need."

"I would hope so. I suppose I'm ready for you to get in touch with that Dellisville couple and make me an appointment. Though I have reservations about some of these claims, I do want to be free. I still have bad dreams, and at times I almost panic without reason. One more thing: the book mentions that some clients experience personality changes afterwards. What if that happens to me, and I end up with alterations to such a degree that you and others lose interest in me?"

He laughed. "I hardly think that's likely. If we should lose interest in each other, I don't think it would be for reasons related to Christian counseling. When are you free to see the Corleys?"

She thought for a minute. "It'll have to be on a Saturday."

"Then what about next Saturday, that is, if they can give you the time?" She nodded affirmatively. He paid the check, and they left, agreeing that he would pick her up at six o'clock for evening church.

* * *

On the drive to Dellisville, Kyle tried making small talk, but Weeda was preoccupied. Sensing her mood, he suggested she recline the seat and try to relax to the tune of some easy-listening music. She agreed but in the same breath complained of butterflies in her stomach.

"That's understandable. You did eat some breakfast, I hope?" She shook her head negatively.

"I asked because those counseling sessions can be lengthy, and a growling gut could prove embarrassing. We'll stop for a bite before we get into town. All I had was some juice and toast."

"Yes, by all means stop if eating will help. My stomach did enough churning last night, and I slept too little. I don't know why I have such a hard time accepting some of those counseling concepts. Why do I?"

"Are you asking yourself or asking me? I mean, do you want my views as to why you're in conflict?"

"If you have that insight, let me have it."

"Possibly it's because you've been partially indoctrinated, and I emphasize partially, with philosophies of the social scientists whose belief systems are often at variance with what the Bible teaches. Since you're a committed Christian, you are pulled between what the Apostle Paul called vain philosophies and the true doctrines of the Bible."

"I can't believe you had such a ready answer."

"Too direct, huh? But am I right?"

"I'm not ready to say, that is, I mean I'm not ready to agree or disagree. Keep talking."

"I don't want to sound judgmental."

"Oh, that's not it... I'm just always wondering what kind of reasoning lies behind all those strong convictions you hold?"

"Reasoning?"

"Yeah! How can you be so sure of yourself?"

"Sure? Of myself?" He emphasized both questions and then added, "Weeda, I make no apologies for the stances I take. I strive to center my thinking and my belief system in the unadulterated truth of the Bible. If I have difficulty with certain passages, I give that difficulty to the Lord and ask for understanding, believing that if I'm incapable of such understanding, then he will enable me to accept the passage as truth even through I fail to comprehend it. He has always been faithful. I also consider as false any teachings of man that run counter to biblical truths. So I hope you'll rethink your question as to my being so sure of myself. My certainties are not centered in myself but in the Scriptures about which I have no misgivings. Quite a distinction, wouldn't you say?"

"Well yes. I suppose I would."

"Good. Glad you could readily agree. I don't want to overdo the preaching."

"Go ahead. I'm getting used to it."

"Sarcasm?"

"I didn't mean to come across that way."

"Do you want to ask specific questions, or shall I, well, pontificate?"

"The latter, I suppose. Do you think I've compromised my Christian beliefs as a result of the studies I've been required to take?"

"Not knowingly. Many Christians practice different types of psychotherapy with varying degrees of success, but for the most part, many of them have accepted without question the theories promoted by so-called experts whose belief systems are steeped in humanism with their anti-Christian philosophies and practices. Their theories, printed and published as fact, have filled the American textbooks for three generations. They have infiltrated and influenced every segment and strata of society, including the Christian churches. Many students who enter college with strong Christian moorings give up their beliefs by accepting the secular and occult teachings of deceived and misguided professors, and they do so without even a questioning pause. It's as easy as slipping off the proverbial greasy log."

Kyle paused and Weeda, shifting the recliner upward, leaned toward him and asked in a quivering, concerned voice, "Do you think I've slipped off that log?"

"I don't think I'm qualified to say. You might get that question answered in today's session."

"Wow! Sounds as though I'm in for an overhaul. Back to your ideas on various theories: Which ones specifically bother you?"

"That's hard to encapsulate since most of the social sciences and their parallel therapies were spawned and have been advanced through the teachings of man whose views of God, of the world, and of the origins of man are not scriptural. Many of the gurus in the field of social science—Freud, for instance—wrote and taught from worldly viewpoints. In their thinking, God doesn't exist. To others, if he does exist, he is unknowable. Still there are others who acknowledge his existence, not as the Creator who superintends his creation, but as one who makes up an integral component of the universe. They contend that nothing outside the world can affect it or change it—that only those substances and entities within the material universe matter. Since to them there is nothing outside the world that can determine values and set standards, then such values and standards do not exist. Such a rationale leaves them free to determine their own values and set their own flexible standards, basing such standards on existing situations and needs. It's upon these fallacious premises that deceived men take the liberty to devise their own guidelines whereby truth becomes relative and gives way to Situational Ethics. What's right and what's wrong varies with the circumstances and conditions. I assume you know full well how I categorize such rubbish?"

"Well yes, and I'm with you on those things. You said the worldly view of man differs from that of a true Christian."

"Weeda, I think you know my thinking along that line."

"Somewhat, but I'd like to hear a rerun."

"Are you sure?"

"Sure, I'm sure. Remember our deal? I'm your sounding board."

"OK. With that in mind, I'll continue. Where were we?"

"You were contrasting the viewpoints about God—the Christian view versus the world view."

"Yes. According to the Bible, the world and things related to it are not without design, and the Designer holds sway by means of spiritual and natural laws that He Himself set in motion. The Designer, the Creator is separate from that which He designed and created and is the final authority for maintaining and upholding all things. He is an entity apart from His creation. His laws are absolutes for which penalties must be paid if violated. For Christians, those are absolutes—black and white, right and wrong. To those who take the opposite view, God is not outside His creation ruling in an overseeing capacity but is one with it. All in God and God in all—monism, one of the basic tenets of the New Agers and their ungodly movements which, by the way, are not new at all but have been around since Nimrod tried to establish his one-world religious empire. These false teachings about the nature of man, the world, and of God Himself have been updated to suit the culture and the times. They have been and continue to be advanced in thousands of psychology classes in nations around the world and are as off-base concerning the nature of man as they are about the world and of God Himself."

"How exactly does your view of man differ from the view of the New Agers?"

"I'll abbreviate because we're not too far from Four Seasons, where we can get some good breakfast food. To begin with, to them man is not a created being brought forth by an omnipotent God but the product of the evolutionary process and is valued because he stands at the zenith, the apex, of that process. So those who subscribe to these teachings and practice their proposed methods are blind to the true nature of man. They discount or deny that he is made in the image of God. They are ignorant of the truth that in the beginning, man, having been made in God's likeness, was endowed with godly attributes and was able to use his faculties to commune with his Creator. Of course, this fellowship was brought to a halt when man sinned. His intellectual powers were diminished and his spirit dulled.

"Though at the time man was mortally wounded, morally damaged, and alienated from God, he still retains the imprint of God's divine image. He is tripartite—having a body, a soul, and a spirit, and much of his striving is rooted in an unconscious urge to be reconciled with his Maker. This drive, this urge is one of the characteristics that defines him as a religious being and separates him from the animals. Through the ages, man has sought something to worship, something to which he can attach and engage his spirit. He can, through the use of his body, interact with the physical and material world. He can engage his soul in intellectual and emotional pursuits, but without a deity, there is nothing to which he can connect his spirit. He lost those moorings when he sinned. Consequently, he seeks to fill that void, and through such seeking he becomes a religious being whether he realizes it or not. Religious pursuits, even those that are pagan, false, and misguided, are still man's feeble effort to fulfill that need for spiritual connection. Augustine had it right when he said something to the effect that man was made for God, and he is restless until he finds that rest in God.

"In summary, social scientists in their textbooks and other venues have failed to address man's most basic need—the need to be reconciled with God. Countless psychology and sociology textbooks have listed and ranked man's basic needs, and no doubt you've had to memorize some of these lists. Have you ever seen man's need for God even suggested in a single one of those lists?" Kyle slowed down, waiting for an answer.

"Uh, no. No such inclusion. So you're saying the social scientists deal only with body and soul?"

"That's what I'm saying. In fact, I know of situations in which clients have asked for spiritual help or insight and were chided by the therapist for having done so. They were accused of using religion as a means of avoiding the prescribed regimen needed for progress. Some therapists see religion as a defense mechanism, a stumbling block to progress. Tied in with this erroneous thinking is the belief that man is born innately good but is corrupted and made evil through negative experiences and hostile environments. Simply put, their remedy lies in altering the environment and conditioning the client. At the highest philosophical levels, these people call themselves behaviorists—B. F. Skinner, for instance. They contend that man through conditioning can evolve to perfection and once they have reached that perfected level, they can continue to enjoy this desired state by maintaining an environment that neither damages nor corrupts but preserves the utopia brought about through the evolutionary and conditioning process. Through the educational humanities and social sciences, these theories have been taught as truth and in countless ways have been an impediment to the Christian cause. Take for instance the myth that every child is born innately good and is marred by his environment. To be sure, society does have corrupting influences and needs drastic changes, but such changes won't solve the sin problem because every child born comes with the seed of sin in his spiritual DNA. Though love, care, and acceptance are requisites for rearing children, only the blood of Jesus can cleanse and eradicate that tendency toward wickedness. These godless myths pertaining to man's innate goodness have served Satan's purposes by negating in the minds of men their need for a savior. Why, in their thinking, do innately good people need a radical change, much less some kind of savior to bring about that change? They just need adjustments that can be attained through psychological therapies. I wish every living person could acknowledge the truth that he is in bondage to his own sinful nature and come to the knowledge that the only available remedy for such an ailment was provided at Calvary 2000 years ago."

Kyle had begun to brake the car as Weeda began to talk. "But Kyle, since I've been converted, and reconciled to God, what..."

"I think I know what you're about to ask and why you're asking it but hold your thought, and we'll deal with it later. We're here at Exit 23, and Four Seasons is just two turns away. This is one of the best dining places in town. Hungry?"

"Not really, but I'll eat anyway. I don't want a growling stomach."

Inside, while Kyle was quietly relishing his scrambled eggs, sausage, and hash browns, Weeda was having lighter fare—French toast with a cup of Constant Comment tea. After several minutes, she broke the silence.

"Kyle, I do so appreciate your coming, your driving me over here. I feel bad that you'll have such a long wait."

"Think nothing of it. I brought my Bible and some reading materials, and besides, from time to time, I'll be praying for you and the counselors."

"I'm so touched. I don't know what to say."

"Then don't try, my dear."

"But I'm so indebted to you."

"That's right, you are. But for now we'll table the thought. One of these days I'll remind you of that indebtedness."

"My, my! What am I letting myself in for?"

"Who knows? But we'll deal with that issue at the right time. For now we'd better be on our way and fast. Look out the window at those rain clouds."

"I can't believe they came up so fast. I'm glad you know where to go."

They arrived at the Christian Care Center just ahead of the storm. The building was an attractive down-home house located in a former residential section of town—an area that had been zoned for business and the houses renovated to serve the needs of the business community. To the left of the Center was Betsy's Beauty Bar, a beauty parlor, and on the right a florist, Plants and Petals.

They rushed from the car and reached the porch just as the downpour started. Kyle rang the doorbell, and a lovely September-Days lady answered. Before Kyle could speak, she said, "I'm Sarah Rogers, the secretary. I remember you. You're Dr. Sanders."

"Yes," Kyle responded, and turning toward Weeda he introduced her. "Ms. Rogers, this is Ms. McVey, Weeda McVey. She has an appointment."

"Yes, the Corleys are expecting her. They have just arrived, so you'll have a short wait. Come on in."

They entered what was once a foyer but now served as a reception area, furnished with a desk and other necessary accessories. Ms. Rogers graciously offered coffee and doughnuts, which they declined, explaining they had just had breakfast at Four Seasons.

"At Four Seasons? Wonderful food, and the atmosphere is so pleasant."

Kyle was agreeing with her and glancing to the right at the same time. He was puzzled. The area that he remembered as the gathering room, a place where groups met for Bible studies and prayer, was empty. Where, he wondered, were the furnishings?

"Oh," said Ms Rogers, sensing his confusion. "I'm sorry this place is in such disarray. We had water damage from a broken pipe and the paper in the two main rooms was ruined, so we're having it redone. The only rooms we can use right now are the back counseling room and the kitchen. The painters are donating their time and services to the ministry, so that explains why they're working on Saturday. We'll be glad to get back to normal."

Kyle needed room while Weeda was in session. Wondering just where he could be quiet and undisturbed, he asked, "Ms. Rogers, can you tell me how to get to the public library? I need a place where I can study and read. I was planning to use your prayer room as I did when I brought that young man down for help, but the library will do."

"Oh, Dr. Sanders, look outside. You can't go out in this storm. Let me make a suggestion. We have a glassed-in back porch with a lounger and chairs. It's comfortable enough, and on a day like this, I don't think you'll be disturbed." He took her up on her offer.

Shortly after Weeda entered the counseling office, Kyle settled himself on the back porch lounger. He opened his briefcase, trying to decide just what he wanted to do first. Should he read and study? Should he relax, or should he pray? Without further delay, he opted for the last. "It's always wise," he mused to himself, "to put prayer first," He closed his briefcase and started praying.

"Dear God, in Your Son's name, I come to the Throne of Grace on behalf of Weeda, Your child, who has been redeemed through that precious blood shed at Calvary. For her redemption, I thank You, but Lord, she needs more of Your grace. Your Word teaches that there are many blessings available through the blessed gift of salvation. It's for this reason that I'm here today. She needs other benefits from the salvation package. She needs deliverance—deliverance from fear, deliverance from guilt. Make her aware that her past sins are truly forgiven so that through that awareness she can more readily forgive others. Also Lord, she needs healing—healing from painful memories, healing of a wounded spirit and a broken heart. Her soul has been scarred though negative experiences, and those scars need to be tenderized so she can be free to love again. Heal the wounds in her heart that could cause her to wound others. I know You can transcend time and space and can through the power of the Holy Spirit loose Weeda from the shackles that hold her in bondage. I believe Your desire to bestow such blessing on us, your children, far exceeds our desire to receive them, so for that reason, I am not reluctant to ask. The knowledge that You're a loving Father who delights in granting the petitions of His anguished and needy children gives me the confidence to seek these blessing for Weeda. I ask that You anoint the counselors and use them as Your instruments to set this captive free. I'm thanking You in advance, and I'll be careful to praise You over and over again as I see these blessings become realities in Weeda's life. Amen. So be it. Amen."

He felt such peace. He closed his eyes and fell asleep.

* * *

Kyle awoke, looked at his watch and realized he had slept almost an hour. It was eleven o'clock. The skies were lighter, but the rain was still coming down. He heard voices punctuated by what sounded like somebody sobbing. Where was it coming from and who was in so much distress? Looking around, he figured it out.

The transom between the porch and the adjacent room was open, and those sounds were coming from the counseling office where Weeda had entered just prior to his settling down on the porch. Those painful cries were coming from Weeda. He recognized her voice and wanted to cry too. Her anguish made him both sad and glad. Sad because she was hurting yet encouraged in the thought that she was being set free from hang-ups that had been holding her in bondage to past hurts and violations. In his medical practice he had learned that heavy weeping was sometimes therapeutic. A twinge of conscience told him he shouldn't be listening, but what was he to do—sit there with his fingers in his ears? The transom control was on the other side. He'd get soaked if he tried to reach the car by exiting the back door and going around the house. Even so, he'd rather get wet than be guilty of eavesdropping, so he tried the doorknob. It was locked, not just latched. He'd disturb the session if he went back through the house. "Oh Lord, I'm trapped."

At that point, he heard Weeda saying between sobs, "But I can't forgive him; I just can't. It's too much."

"Why can't you forgive him?"

"Because I was entitled to a father. He robbed me of having a father."

"You resent the fact that you had to grow up without a father?"

"Wasn't I entitled to a father?"

"Every child deserves to be loved and cared for by two parents, that's for sure, but because parental and corporate sins are so rampant, too few are. I believe you said you were five and your brother was seven when he disappeared. Many people can recall experiences they had at that age. What, if anything, do you remember about your father?"

"I'm not sure. There are many things in my head about him, but I have trouble separating what I actually experienced from what I've been told or heard discussed."

"That's understandable. It might be helpful if you'd share what's in your head, as you put it."

"There is one experience I can definitely put in the memory category."

"Can you share it?"

"I remember my dad saying goodbye as he was leaving for what Mother said was an appointment to see the doctor. Sammy and I were out in the yard playing, and on his way to the car he brushed by us. He tousled Sammy's hair and reached down and kissed me on top of the head. Mom said she was watching out the window when this happened, and that's the last time we saw him."

"Did he see the doctor after he left, or do you know?"

"Yes, there is evidence that he did see the doctor, but nothing is known beyond that."

"Surely there was an investigation?"

"Yes, but nothing ever turned up. His medical records furnished no clues."

"Did your mother know why he was seeing the doctor?"

"It was his yearly check-up, so all recordings were nothing more than routine procedures—blood pressure reading and that type of thing."

"Was your mother satisfied with the investigation?"

"Definitely not. She has always believed Dr. Hall knows something, but she has no way to prove it. She could not collect insurance since there was never a verification of death, and she was not financially able to hire private investigators. Dr. Hall is a respected and capable physician, though he is getting ready to retire, and so this mystery remains just that—a mystery."

"What do you think? Do you think he met with foul play?"

After a long silence and continued weeping, she sobbed. "I almost wish I could believe that. It would be less painful than what I've come to fear."

"What do you believe? Explain."

"I can't bring myself to say it."

"Are you afraid he disappeared by choice?"

"I wonder. I just don't know, but there's something in me that resents him."

"Yes, that's evident and insightful on your part. In your work, you deal with human emotions. Surely you've tried to figure out why you are so resentful."

"Yes, I've thought about it much too much, I'm afraid. As I've already said, he robbed my brother and me of a fatherly relationship, and I emphasize robbed. We both thought he was Superman and could accomplish whatever he wanted. In our minds, if he had wanted to come home to us nothing could have prevented his return."

"Sammy is older than you?"

"Yes, by two years. He was seven at the time."

"So in your child's mind, he deserted the family?"

"I suppose that sums it up."

"How about in your adult thinking?"

"I've tried to think—I want to believe differently."

"Good, but that's your intellect working, not your emotions, and sad to say it's your emotions that dictate your attitude, your reactions, and your behavior even in your day-to-day relationships, especially toward men, yes?"

"You may be right. I'm still amazed that I was able to fall in love with Lanny and bring myself to marry him."

"And then that bad experience added to your problems?"

"I can accept that, but what do I do about it?"

"We'll get to that shortly, but let's talk about your feelings a bit more. I wonder if what you call resentment might be a euphemism for something else that you really feel?"

"Such as?"

"Hatred...hatred that maybe turned into bitterness?"

"Hatred? I hope not. Bitterness? Possibly, but it hasn't always been a factor."

There was a pause, and Kyle wondered if Weeda could answer that question. Did she know when the bitterness set it? Finally, he heard her say, "When I learned that Lanny was bisexual."

"You connected some dots?" he heard Corley say in a questioning tone.

"Maybe that's what I did, but I wasn't aware of it. Now that I'm talking to you, I can understand why you might see it that way."

"Maybe those dots were a figment of your imagination with no connection to reality?"

"You may be right, but regardless of how much I pray, I can't dismiss the suspicion that my dad was bisexual and left his family for a male lover. I'd give anything to get those thoughts out of my mind. These particular thoughts had never tormented me until my marriage to Lanny failed. I think that's when I became bitter. Also, I want to add that the work I do seems to keep these personal problems ever before me. If I had training in any other field, I'd leave counseling. At this stage, it's so impractical to start studying in another discipline."

"The personal counseling gets to you?"

"I must say. I enjoy the academic and career guidance, but parent-child relationships do get to me."

"Sounds as though you have to deal with some thorny situations."

"Yes, one in particular, and I'm having a hard time dealing with it head on."

"Hurts?"

"Very. In fact, at times I'm afraid to deal with it."

"That's understandable, but changing jobs won't solve your problems. Wherever you go, you'll take these hang-ups with you. You're in bondage to fear, which you yourself have addressed. Hatred, resentment, and bitterness are heavy burdens to bear, and since you're a committed Christian and know it's wrong to hate, guilt sets it and compounds the bondage. I'm sure it takes a great deal of energy just to keep the lid on."

"Indeed it does, but what do I do about it?"

"As an act of your will and through the power of the Holy Spirit, you ask God to forgive you for allowing hatred to take over, and then you outwardly express your forgiveness toward your dad. Bow your head and pray from your heart something to that effect, just as you did when we dealt with your feelings toward Lanny."

At that point, Weeda stopped crying and was speaking softly so that her prayer was not audible to Kyle. The rain had let up, and as he stood up again, he saw a key hanging on the outer edge of the door facing. Why had he not noticed it before? Resisting the temptation to listen longer, he unlocked the door and quickly found his way to his car out front.

* * *

On the drive back to Rushton, Weeda sat quietly and wept. Noticing that she had used all the Kleenex, Kyle fumbled it his pocket, pulled out a hanky and placed it in her hands. At the same time, he gave her a pat on the knee, indicating his concern.

"Thank you, Kyle. Please don't think I'm crying because I'm sad. I just can't stop crying."

"I understand. No explanation necessary."

"The truth is, I've never felt lighter. I can't explain it, but the tears just keep coming. I can't stop crying."

"Don't try. Give in to your feelings."

"I'm not sure what my feelings are. I know I'm not the same."

"That's good. It means you've had a measure of success. It may take several days for you to get adjusted to this new-found freedom."

"That's what the Corleys said. Kyle, they were—well—full of the Spirit of God. I was amazed at their abilities to deal with my problems—feelings and emotions I didn't even know were troubling me."

Kyle smiled and nodded knowingly. "Those abilities, my dear, are not necessarily innate to the Corleys but gifts that come with the anointing which the Holy Spirit furnishes to his servants as they work his Will. It's an awesome thing to experience or observe the Holy Spirit in action."

"Indeed it is. It truly is. I'll never doubt your theology again. When you tell me something, I'll accept it."

"Now wait a minute. I appreciate your confidence, but not trust to that extent. Just because I'm right about some things doesn't mean I'm right about all things. I speak emphatically about the reliability of the Scriptures because I believe them to be inerrant, but I can be off in my interpretation of certain passages; therefore, I'm not offended when you or anyone else checks the Word for the purpose of discounting or verifying my interpretations. In fact, we are told to do just that. Remember the Bereans? They went to the Scriptures concerning the teachings of the Apostle Paul and were commended for doing so. Check it out in the Book of Acts, but not today. I should think you've had enough such involvement for now. Are you hungry?"

"Not exactly hungry, but empty. I know you must be starved, unless you ate something while you were waiting."

"No, I had a cup of coffee with Ms. Rogers about one o'clock when the rain let up."

"Did it rain that long? Did you get some reading done?"

That question put Kyle on the spot. He certainly didn't intend at this time to let her know he had overheard a very sensitive portion of the counseling session, so he stammered, "I...I...well, for one thing I caught up on some much needed sleep. That lounge was so comfortable. After praying for you and the Corleys, I gave in to my feelings, and that steady rain lulled me off to sleep."

"I'm glad you got some rest."

"Speaking of rest, usually people need additional sleep after such a lengthy work-out as you had today. Though you say you feel relieved, I should think you must be weary."

"A work-out was what I had all right. Some of it was really hard to deal with."

"I'm sorry it was rough on you, but you'll benefit in the long run."

"I do want to talk with you about certain aspects of it, but not today."

"Sure, of course, but give yourself some time." He could see that her head had begun to nestle into her neck pillow, and she was falling asleep. He put the speedometer on cruise control, expecting to reach Rushton in about an hour.

When the alarm went off at seven, Weeda sleepily reached over and banged it off. She wasn't at all in the frame of mind to get going. She had slept soundly but felt the need for more rest. As she changed positions, she realized it was Sunday and half-aloud mumbled to herself, "To go or not to go." Then half prayerfully, "Lord, this is Sunday, Your day, and I should honor You with my presence at church, but I need more time to mull over what happened to me yesterday. The hurry and scurry of getting to church and back plus the social interaction while there will not allow me any time for reflection. Forgive me if I'm rationalizing, but Your word exhorts us to be still and know that You are God. Today I would like to be obedient to that command. I'd like to spend this day in quiet gratitude and prayer. Eventually, I want to share more of yesterday's experience with Kyle, but not today. Will You orchestrate his time so he doesn't call?

"The fact that I don't want to hear from him is a bit frightening. Both he and the Corleys have said I might have a new self-image or something to that effect. Lord, if I am a changed person, and I think I am, I don't want my interest in Kyle to lessen with the change. No...no... no. That's too much change. So my request that Kyle not call is temporary, for today only. This newfound freedom is great, but I don't want to lose Kyle in the process. Thank You for understanding this confusing prayer."

She slipped into her robe and went into the kitchen. A cup of tea with toast and apple butter might help get her started. While the tea was brewing, she continued her mulling. It was amazing how the Corleys had led her to pray in ways she had never prayed before, and the results were astounding. She no longer hated her father, and the anger was gone, not only toward him but also toward herself.

She had actually forgiven herself for having married Lanny. The relationship with him had been a disaster but one she could put behind her—an experience that she now believed would cease to impact her present and future behavior. Wow! What a relief!

She sipped her tea and kept wondering. Why did the churches not utilize this kind of ministry to set their church members free? Suddenly there came to mind the names of several people who could benefit from this kind of help. Topmost in her mind were Sonny and his father. She'd start praying to that end, that somehow they would avail themselves of this ministry. Why not ask Kyle to join her in that prayer? On second thought, such an agreement would necessitate discussing the whole sordid affair with him. Could or should she do that? She felt the Lord was giving her a go-ahead green light.

* * *

While driving to school on Monday morning, Weeda realized her Sunday morning prayer had surely been answered. Kyle had not called, but she wasn't so sure she was as pleased as she thought she'd be. She would have welcomed a late-night chat. Now she was wondering why. Maybe she should have called him. She had asked God for a quiet uninterrupted day, and he had given her the evening too.

She was approaching the school grounds, so her thoughts shifted. One thing was for sure—she felt free and energetic. Would anybody notice the change? She felt so different; so how could she look the same? If someone mentioned the change, what would she say? How could she explain? She certainly wanted to give God the glory, the credit. But how do you do that when the listener has little or no frame of reference for understanding such spiritual things? Most of the people she knew fell into that category. She knew the barriers to perceiving things of the spirit because she herself had just begun to emerge from that world of blindness and ignorance. She'd have to ask Kyle about how to share these newfound truths and experiences.

A few minutes later, she settled herself at her desk and scanned her weekly calendar. It was all sprinkled with meetings, student appointments, and parental conferences. "Oh my!" she said aloud, "here's Hammie's name for 10:30. What's he gotten into now?" The question brought a smile. Even though the boy was an annoyance, he was a rarity—void of pretense and guile, and his predicaments furnished freshness and sometimes comic relief from the everyday humdrum. Those pleasant thoughts were immediately offset when she saw Cody Houston's name inserted in the 2:00 slot for Thursday. Her buzzer sounded; the day had begun. "Lord," she prayed, "guide me this day, and let the words of my mouth bring no reproach to Your name."

At 10:30, Hammie walked into the office and took a seat.

"Hi, Hammie. I haven't seen you lately."

"Nome. That's 'cause I ain't been in no trouble."

"Good. I'm glad you came to tell me about it. I like such reports."

"Not so fast. I said ain't been, not 'still am'."

"What do you mean?"

"I mean I wuz doin' just fine tit I run afoul with Miz White in study hall last Friday."

"What kind of trouble?

"For talkin' too much so she said, so she's makin' me take the school handbook and write down all the rules."

"Well, that's not such a bad idea. Things stick in our minds better when we write them down."

"Yeah, once, maybe so, but ten times? It don't take no ten times for me to get sumpin to stick in my noggin."

"Ten times?" She hoped her expression didn't reflect what she was thinking. "Have you finished the assignment?"

"Not even half done. There's more'n a dozen rules, you know. I'm just on round five."

"Do you have a deadline?"

"That's why I'm here. I'm sposed to turn 'em in at fifth period today, but I went fishin' Saturday and wuz in church twice Sunday, so I didn't have a bit of time to write. I thought you might could splain to her why I'm not even half done and while you're at it you could tell her why it's necessary for me to talk in study hall."

"I don't understand. Why do you feel you should have that privilege?"

"Well, you see it's like this: I'm in Mr. Doyle's Bible class three times a week. He's been teachin' on the Holy Spirit. First, he told us all about the Fruits of the Spirit. Then he started on the Gifts. He said, and I honest to God believe him, that God gives every Christian a gift. He said we have to use whatever gift He gives us, that we gotta practice it, and that's zackly what I've been tryin' to do."

"Hammie, I don't get it. What does that have to do with talking in study hall?"

"Everything. You see, I have the gift of encouragement, and I feel real special 'cause I have this gift, but I try not to make a big to-do about it. I'm just tryin' to do what Mr. Doyle said and what God specks. Now I ask you, Miz McVey, how can I encourage my friends if I'm not 'lowed to talk to 'em?"

* * *

That evening after dinner, Weeda enjoyed a leisurely bath then settled down with Spurgeon's *Book of Sermons*. His writings always seemed to balance her mainspring and put things in perspective. She finished his sermon on the Doctrine of Faith then picked up the Handbook of Christian Counseling the Corleys had given her, which they felt might be helpful in her school work. As she thumbed through it, she kept thinking how good it would be if some of the methods and techniques could be utilized at RCS, so she uttered a little prayer to that effect: "Dear Lord, I would like to see this ministry established here at Rushton. If this in accordance with Your will, then give me the courage to initiate such a program and open doors for such a ministry." At that moment, the telephone rang. It was Kyle.

"Hi Weeda! Things going OK?"

"I think so. No, I'll modify that, I know so."

"Good. Just checking to see how you're doing. Been sleeping and reflecting?"

"Well, not today since I was busy at school, but that's exactly what I did yesterday, and by evening I was ready to talk to you."

"Then why didn't you call?"

"No one reason I can think of."

"To be honest, I intended to give you a ring last night, but I got so absorbed in my reading materials, and midnight came before I knew it."

"What's your focus now? The Second Coming?"

"Right. It's amazing that so many prophecies are being fulfilled right before our eyes. Almost every news report relays some situation significant to end time prophecies. These happenings are signs of the times, but sad to say, the average church member doesn't recognize them as relevant to his Christian walk."

"I'm ready to hear more. Have you reached a decision about the timing of the Rapture?"

"Sure have."

"Well, which one? I like the Pre-trib, you know."

"Of course. Who doesn't? But according to Jesus, the Apostle Paul and the Prophet John, we don't have options. Scriptures teach that the taking away of the saints follows the Tribulation but precedes the Day of the Lord. The Day of the Lord is that period of time when God pours out His wrath on the ungodly, those left after he has raptured the saints. This 'taking up' comes immediately after the Tribulation. Read Revelation 7:14 and following."

"You amaze me. How have you managed to come to such definite conclusions so soon? You've been into this study only a few weeks and already you're taking issue with scholars who have given a lifetime to the study of eschatology."

"I'm fully aware of that and discussing these things with you is probably premature on my part. Further study may cause me to modify my views, so what I'm telling you is not for publication."

"I understand, but for now, you've piqued my curiosity about the Rapture. What Scripture led you to negate the Pre-trib theory? I know you're not Post-trib. So that leaves Mid-trib, yes?"

"Almost right—not quite."

"What do you mean, almost right, not quite? You're the one who emphasizes absolutes—right and wrong, no gray."

"OK, let me explain. The Tribulation is that period of time when Satan vents his wrath against mankind, especially against the saints of God. His persecutions begin with Daniel's Seven-year Covenant. This period will continue for approximately three and one-half years. At that time the Antichrist reneges on his agreement and declares himself to be God, soliciting the worship of mankind. That passage is found in 2 Thes. 1:4-5."

"Hold it. I'm jotting all this down."

After a pause, "Got it?"

"Yes, go ahead."

"Some time after the Antichrist declares his deity, God will rapture his elect, and the Day of the Lord commences. Paul gives a view of the Rapture in 1 Thes. 4:13-17 and in 1 Cor. 15:51-52. The Day of the Lord takes up the remaining three and one-half years of Daniel's seven-year period and possibly extends beyond that time. This phase of the Day of the Lord climaxes with the Battle of Armageddon when Satan is bound for a thousand years. Following that great and terrible battle, God will start a reclamation process followed by a period of restoration wherein the earth, the planet itself, will be redeemed. That, my dear, is a condensed summary of a condensed summary. It's not difficult to understand if you define correctly the Day of the Lord and separate Satan's wrath during the Tribulation from the time of God's wrath which ushers in the Day of the Lord."

"Whoops! I'm not sure I can take all this in, but I have one more question while we're on this topic. Remember the evangelist who conducted the revival a few months ago? I can't remember his name. Anyway, he kept referring to the imminency of Christ's return. I think that's the term he used, meaning he could come at any moment. I recall you questioned the concept at the time. Have you changed your mind?"

"No, in fact my readings have confirmed what I've thought all along—that Christ's return is not imminent because the Antichrist has not yet been revealed. The truth is made known by Paul in his Second letter to the Thessalonians, 2 Thess. 2:2-3. That one passage is sufficient to offset any notion about the imminency of Christ's return. After the AC declares himself to be God, then Christ's return will become imminent. My sounding board becoming weary?"

"Definitely not. You've whetted my appetite. Now I'm torn. Should I read these prophetic passages or should I go back to my handbook on counseling?"

"Aha! Already I'm seeing the results of Saturday's session. I think you're coming into that hunger and thirst you indicated you lacked. Agree?"

"You may be right. Maybe I'll be able to read the Bible with more understanding."

"I'll let you get back to your handbook or go to the Scripture passages, whichever, and I'll talk with you tomorrow evening."

They said goodnight and Weeda was left to ponder the many things in her heart.

* * *

Cody Houston arrived on time for his appointment, but Weeda was on the phone with the Director of Family Services so he had to wait. Finally, she asked him in and was aghast at his appearance. As always, he was well groomed and appropriately dressed. That was not it. It was his countenance—all taunt, heavy, and downcast. She had to resist the impulse to express concern.

He started talking as he entered the door. "I'm grateful for your time, Ms. McVey. As you know, I'm here to, uh, well, to discuss Sonny again."

"Yes, I've been expecting a follow-up. In our last discussion, you were concerned about his unusual behavior. Have you observed any change?"

"I wish I could give a good report, but sorry to say, that's not the case. He's still aloof, sulky, spaced-out."

"I'm sorry. Are you two talking at all?"

"Very little, and when we do, it's as though we're strangers."

"What about your wife? Is he behaving toward her in a similar manner?"

"About the same, and it's breaking her heart."

"Have you confronted him and asked for an explanation?"

"Well no, I haven't."

"Still afraid?"

"That's it," he said, his voice shaking and his hands trembling.

"You're still fearful that such a confrontation might lead to a discussion of the adoption?"

"I'm afraid to risk the possibility."

"If unearthing the truth proved to be so devastating, who would suffer the consequences?"

"I would. I would. I'm highly suspicious that Sonny knows something about his birth parents."

"So Mr. Houston, there is something about his birth that if known is a real threat to you?"

"Right. There is, and the whole thing is crashing down on me. I hope you can help me."

"I'm not asking you to disclose anything you might later regret, but it seems you're not able to discipline your son because such discipline might lead to an exposure you're not wanting to face. You've become vulnerable and the vulnerability renders you impotent as a disciplinarian and as a father."

"You're so right, but I don't know what to do about it. It's the first time in my life I've ever been nonplused, immobilized. I've always had a sense of direction and knew fairly well how to steer my activities so I could realize my goals, but this is different. I can't see my way out. I'm in a bind."

"You're an active church member, so I assume you're a practitioner of the faith—that you have a relationship with Jesus Christ, not just playing church as some people do?"

There was a lull in the conversation. Weeda continued to look straight at him, but he avoided her eyes. He grew pale, became quiet, and encircled his jaws in the palm of his hands, resting his head in a downward gaze. Finally, he removed his hands, lifted his head and reopened the dialogue.

"Ms. McVey, I'm not the man I appear to be, but I don't know how, I don't know how, how to say it."

"Take your time; I'll wait."

"I do play church, as you put it, but tell me if you can, how can I quit playing when setting things straight would bring ruination to my family, possibly to my business, and certainly to my standing in the community?"

Something came over Weeda and she commenced to utter thoughts that didn't exactly belong to her mindset but were nevertheless emanating from her mouth. "I don't know what's in your background, but this I do know: it's better to risk ruination in the eyes of the world than to suffer your soul's damnation in the hands of God's judgment. Have you prayed about this crisis?"

"I've tried, but my words go nowhere."

"But I've heard you give lovely offertory prayers at church."

He registered shock at her candid remarks but managed to say, "I'm afraid I've prepared those prayers for the benefit of the listening congregation with little or no concern about what God thought, and now God's not interested in what I have to say."

"Oh, I see! You're worried about your relationship with Sonny, and well you should be, but seems to me you've been neglecting a relationship that's ever so much more vital, your relationship with the Lord, Jesus Christ. Perhaps you need to make things right with Him before you attempt to make things right with Sonny. In fact, making things right with Him may be the prerequisite to making things right with your son."

"What if that's impossible?"

"Nothing is impossible with God."

"No doubt you're right about God's part, but what about my part? I don't know how to do my part. Do you?"

"Yes, I do. For a start and as an act of your will, you must make a confession of your sins, asking God's forgiveness and accepting his pardon. Following that you must forgive all those people who you believe have wronged you."

"Maybe I've heard that message from the pulpit, but I've never taken it personally, and I feel so awkward even discussing it for myself."

"I understand. Would you consider allowing some professional Christian counselors to help you?"

"Who? Where? I can't confide in anybody far or near, not even the preacher." Then he looked at her with a flickering idea. "You're a counselor and also a Christian. What's to prevent you from helping? I would trust you."

Weeda was floored and momentarily regretted her suggestion. She was thinking of engaging the Corleys for the task—surely not Weeda McVey. At that moment there flashed through her mind a recent petition she herself had made: "Dear God, if it's Your will, will You open doors to establish a prayer-counseling ministry at RCS?" Somehow, she knew God was in this and was responsible for the flashback, so she responded with another prayer: "Father, let the Holy Spirit take the lead here."

"I'll have to give that request some thought. For such an endeavor, we'd need a block of time outside regular school hours. I'll certainly make it a matter of prayer. In the meantime, take heart. God does answer prayer. The fact that you're here today is proof of that fact."

"Thank you, Ms. McVey." As he was leaving, he turned and hoarsely whispered, "Please pray that I don't seek some foolish way to bring an end to this seemingly hopeless situation." With that he departed.

Just what was he implying? The thought puzzled her. She couldn't wait to get Kyle's input on everything that had gone on between her and Cody Houston.

"Oh my!" she said aloud, "my club meets tonight, but I wouldn't hesitate to beg off if Kyle could come over." She rang his number, something she was reluctant to do, but this was no ordinary situation. She needed his advice immediately. The desk attendant answered, saying she'd ask Dr. Sanders to return her call between patients.

Thirty minutes later Kyle called back. "Hi Weeda. What's up?"

"Kyle, are you free this evening?"

"Well, yes and no. I'll be tied up until almost nine. After that my time is yours if you need me, and I'm assuming from this call that you do. Is nine too late?"

"I'll take you any time I can get you."

"Good, I'm recording that statement so I can hold you to it. Are you all right?"

"Physically, yes, but I'm in a quandary. I have to make some decisions about the Houston case."

"Things coming to a head?"

"Not yet, but God is working. Kyle, I'm way, way over my head and short on expertise."

"Weeda, if God is in this, and you say He is, let me assure you that you're not over your head. Just trust and obey. I'll see you about nine. I'm running a tight schedule, so do me a favor? Have me a snack ready."

"I'll do better than that. I'll prepare dinner."

* * *

When Kyle arrived, the food was ready—braised lamb chops with mint sauce, steamed wild rice, glazed carrots, and a congealed fruit salad. She purposely delayed a discussion of the Houston case so he could enjoy the meal, so she tried peppering in some small manufactured talk, but Kyle was ready to deal with the problem.

"So you're over your head, eh? Tell me about it."

"Houston came in today even more concerned about Sonny and the adoption issue. In fact, he was visibly distraught, and as it turned out, the discussion about Sonny ended out on the periphery, and Houston himself became the center—the focus of the conference."

"What brought that on?"

"Whatever Sonny learned about his birth has been devastating to the boy, and now his dad is in a state of depression brought on by anxiety, I suppose. He suspects Sonny has learned some secrets about his birth parents, and that fear is incapacitating the man."

"And you don't know what those secrets are?"

"No, I've never asked nor have I thrown out any feelers to find out. I have avoided fishing for that info. I'll admit I'm fearful—afraid I'll learn something that will somehow make me an accomplice to whatever. Surely those secrets must involve deeds that are unlawful, illegal, immoral. Maybe all three. I say that because the man is literally scared to death of an exposure. But there does appear to be a ray of hope: his fears are driving him toward God. He wants His help but he says he doesn't know how to make contact."

"He can't make contact with God? Uh, um, makes you wonder about his redemption."

"Exactly. He admits he's a pseudo and has been playing church all these years."

"Sounds as though God might be using the situation to give the man an opportunity to get saved."

"Hopefully, something good is in the making. He's begging for help. Says he doesn't know how to pray even though I've heard him render the offertory prayer several times in church. I can't explain what happened, but before I knew it, I was suggesting prayer counseling or something equivalent to it. I had the Corleys in mind."

"Good, so you want me to make the arrangements?"

"That's what I'd like, but that's not the way it turned out. When I explained the initial stages for getting to know God—confession of sins and all that, his response caught me off guard when he said he'd confide and confess if I'd help him. I was floored and ready to make a referral, but the Holy Spirit didn't allow me to refuse. So you see where I am. I was preparing him to see the Corleys but..."

Kyle laughed. "Yes, I see through it very well. What you meant for the Corleys, God has assigned to you. That's God for you."

"Kyle, it's not funny. Where do I go from here?"

"I'm not laughing at you. It's just delightful to see how God works. My suggestion is that you arrange a time for prayer and counseling, but not alone."

"Yeah, I remember the manual's guidelines."

"You'll need to explain those regulations to Houston—that prayer counseling is not a one-on-one, but small group work. You'll need a partner."

"Good. That's where you come in."

"Maybe so. Maybe not. He knows me, but not professionally. If he feels uncomfortable with my presence, then we'll make other arrangements."

"So, the Holy Spirit has locked me into this situation, but thankfully, he's locking you in with me."

"Could be, so set it up."

"It'll have to be on a Saturday. Where? At school?"

"Don't you think my office would be a better place? Nothing goes on there on Saturday afternoons."

Weeda went to bed soon after Kyle left and fell asleep immediately, so relieved that he was in this boat with her.

* * *

The next morning Weeda put a priority on making arrangements for helping Cody—the sooner the better. Both the Lord and the devil were making a bid for his soul, and she and Kyle were agreeing in prayer on the side of the Lord. Finding a block of time when the three could get together was the problem.

After several calls back and forth from Kyle's office to Cody's, the time was set a week from Saturday at two o'clock. That was a longer wait than they had wanted, but it was the best they could do. Kyle was on call for the coming weekend, and Weeda had insisted on his involvement. At first, Cody had resisted meeting with Kyle, not for any particular reason except that he wanted to confine his sharing to only one person. But she gave him no choice: include Kyle or call off the deal. Cody conceded.

She gave a sigh of relief at having accomplished this much. Hopefully, she could now turn her attention to other things, but in checking her schedule from the desk calendar, she realized this was just wishful thinking, for there she saw Macy's name in one of the slot columns. It seemed she was meeting one of the Houstons at every turn, but as for this afternoon, there would be a change.

The T Group—short for Therapy—was made up of pupils who were always getting into trouble, not serious infractions, just pupil-teacher run-ins that Mr. Drago felt could be avoided if pupils and teachers could talk informally and get to know one another outside the classroom. He himself had compiled the list; using as a guide those pupils who had frequented his office on teacher referrals but who he felt were merely making bids for attention and were using misbehavior to get it. He reasoned that giving them a block of time for expressing their thoughts and venting their feelings might get them over that 'Mama, Mama, look at me' syndrome. Naturally, being the counselor, Weeda was chosen as the therapist.

This was the group's third meeting so she needed to get prepared. In looking over the T-Group folder, she noticed Hammie Hank's name had been added and wondered how he had escaped inclusion thus far. The thought brought a smile to her otherwise serious demeanor, and to herself she mumbled, "Hammie, the boy who thinks in tune with his inner self but to others sounds off-key."

One by one the group sauntered into the guidance office and by 3:30 had taken their places around the conference table. Mr. Adams, the general science teacher, sat at one end and Weeda at the other. She checked the attendance against the roster of names. All were present except one—Hammie Hanks.

"Oh my!" she thought, "what's happened now?" She knew the director of transportation had made arrangements to get him home afterwards, so what was his excuse for not showing up? She couched her concern by saying, "We'll get started and not wait for Hammie. He'll be here shortly, I'm sure."

The group members talked back and forth for the first few minutes about sports, the football team, what they liked and disliked, what changes needed to be made. Some thought the players were too privileged and shouldn't be. Others disagreed, feeling the players provided pleasure for the students and community and should be permitted some entitlements. Their attitudes ranged the gamut. Jack was hostile. Sam was angry. Erleen was a show-off. Later they discussed the school lunch program and wrote down their suggestion for improvements that Weeda promised to turn over to the food manager.

She was getting more concerned about Hammie and excused herself to check on him. When she returned, the discussion had shifted and was centered on the school's dress code, a subject they had previously discussed but one which whetted their appetites for participation. Looking at her watch, she realized the time was almost up and was giving Mr. Adams the signal to wind down when in walked Hammie. Weeda caught his eye and silently pointed to the empty seat, fully expecting him to be seated without interrupting the discussion. He did take the seat but not quietly.

"Ms. McVey, I need to tell you why I missed this here session," to which Weeda nodded with a negative shake of her head, but Hammie ignored the gesture and kept talking. There it was again— the boy's ability to get and keep people's attention. It was hard to explain. He was non-descriptive in appearance and his comments imparted little knowledge, if any, but people listened when Hammie spoke. When he interjected his thoughts, he took center stage, and teachers temporarily took a back seat. And so it was this afternoon.

"You see, that history teacher sent me to detention again. Just like always, I couldn't see why. That's where I've been—in the Big D."

"OK, Hammie, we're about to finish, so we'll discuss that later."

He ignored her comment and kept on talking. "Beats me why she sent me there. She said I wuz not respectin' her, but for the life of me, I can't see that sayin' what needs to be said is bad. We wuz takin' a test and I wuz tryin' to finish up the last question and she got all bent out of shape 'cause I was slow.

"She yelled at me and said, 'Hammie, you try my patience. I've been watchin' you, and you just set there doin' nothing—not just once but just settin' there time on end.' She hit the ceiling when I told her I didn't have nothing else besides my end that I could set on."

They all heehawed as they left the room.

* * *

Macy was late for her appointment, and frustration was written all over her face and evident in her voice. "I'm sorry I'm late." She took a seat and continued: "The yearbook photographer is taking pictures, and it's so hard to get every thing to dovetail and keep schedules exactly on time. Something happened to a roll of film and he had to do a retake of the yearbook staff."

"I understand. It's not always easy to control one's timing, especially when mechanical equipment is involved."

"Thanks for being understanding. I have several things I want to talk to you about."

"Sure, let's get started. I have several minutes. How can we best use them?"

"For one thing, I wanted to give you a report on the progress we're making toward the Bible study we've been praying about. We now have about thirty students signed up, the majority from public schools, and the offer is still open."

"Macy, that's wonderful. I feel bad that you've done so much of this work alone."

"No problem. Since it was announced, the response has been good. As specified, the calls come in during early evening and Mom takes them. She answers questions, explains the plan and registers those who are interested. Those signed up are counting on a Saturday morning class. If it's held at any other time, some will have to drop out."

"Of course. Now we'll have to firm up some other things. I'm hoping Dr. Sanders will do the instruction. He's praying about it. In the event he has to decline, we've arranged for a couple from Dellisville to teach. I'm so glad you came in with such good news I was afraid you were here to talk about..."

"Sonny?" To which Weeda nodded, and Macy continued her remarks. "Well, to be honest, that is my main reason for coming. The Bible study was incidental."

"Oh?"

"Yes, Sonny and I have split, and I'm broken hearted, but my parents insisted that I not see him anymore. I suppose I can't blame them. Sonny's such a disappointment."

"Anything I don't know about?"

"You probably know more than I do. I have two classes with him, and I sense that the teachers are baffled. Mrs. Houston has had conferences with them. I know about them because she has called me, so concerned about the way he has changed. I would like to remain friends with Sonny and be able to help him, but I feel I must obey my parents."

"By all means. Have you talked to Sonny's father?"

"Yes, just a few days ago. He called, wanting me to persuade Sonny to register for the Bible study, but I explained to him the situation with my parents. He said he was sorry our friendship was ending."

"What's Sonny doing now? I haven't talked to him lately. He didn't show up for his last appointment that his parents scheduled through Ms. Larson. We did notify them of his failure to show. Do you still believe he has a drug problem?"

"I just don't know. He's really weird—so strange."

"How's he responding to your break-up?"

"He said he wasn't surprised and added that his life was headed downhill and it wasn't fair to take me down with him. I must admit I've been shaken up, but I do have to move on. His parents have even tried to get out-of-town medical help for him, but he has refused."

"Um—did you say, out of town?"

"That's what they told me—outside the state. I don't know the reasons for going so far, but anyway, they said he wouldn't consent to it."

"Well, Macy, our time is up. Thanks for working on the Bible study plans, and we'll keep praying for Sonny. God can do even the impossible. Let's be encouraged in that thought. There are some things happening which I'm not free to share, but are nevertheless positive signs."

"Thanks! I needed to hear that. I can't wait to hear more. I'll run now, but I'll be back as soon as you can see me."

* * *

On Saturday afternoon while driving to Kyle's office to meet with Cody, Weeda prayed. "Lord, I'm nervous. I don't think it's because I'm doing prayer counseling for the first time. If it were anybody else, I wouldn't be so jittery, but Cody Houston? You know I dread what's coming up. I dread the possibility of an outcome that just might take on a life of its own—one that I don't feel qualified to handle. I still think Mr. Drago should be in on this case, but, well, you know Cody balked on that. Lord, I thank you that Kyle is taking the lead. Do enable him to lean on the Holy Spirit for wisdom and enable me to help, not hinder in any way. Your Word admonishes us to give thanks in all things, so in obedience to that command, I am thanking You in advance for the upcoming experience and for what You are going to do in Cody's life. In the name of Jesus I make these requests. Amen."

When she arrived at the office, Mr. Houston was in the waiting room filling out papers—information forms Kyle had obtained from the Corleys. The questions, when answered, provided the counselors a background sketch of the counselee's spiritual beliefs and experiences, of his relationships to family members and other authority figures, and connections, if any, to false religions, and any involvements in any illegal, unlawful, or immoral activities. Also, counselees were asked to list situations in which they had been sinned against—the times they felt they had been victimized.

Weeda could see that Cody was concentrating on the forms, so she passed him by and joined Kyle in his consultation room where they joined in prayer for Cody and his situation. Finally, having finished the forms, Cody entered the inner office. Immediately, Weeda noticed that his countenance was different from what she had remembered in her office the day he was asking for help. He had taken on a self-assured air. What, she wondered, had transpired to account for the change? They had talked on the phone just yesterday. At that time, the tone of his voice and the tenor of the conversation certainly didn't match what she was observing. Naturally, she didn't mention the change but nevertheless was impatient for an explanation. Was he going to renege and not cooperate? She'd soon find out.

At Kyle's suggestion, Cody took a seat facing them from across the desk. They were taken aback when he pointed to the forms and said, "I can't believe it's necessary to invade a person's privacy to this degree, just to help solve a personal problem."

Though stunned, Weeda came back with, "I wasn't aware you were here merely to discuss a personal problem. When you talked with me, you wanted something more—a relationship with Jesus Christ. There's a difference. Seeking help with a personal problem and getting to know Christ, though they can be intertwined, are not synonymous." Kyle nodded in support and Weeda continued. "I grant you, you do have a problem—a father-son relationship, but if I recall correctly, you came to the conclusion that restoring your relationship with your son just might hinge on your first establishing a relationship with the Lord. Is that what you remember?"

"Uh, well, yes, but I didn't have any idea such an effort would require me to reveal all the ins and outs of my personal life."

Kyle spoke up. "You're partially right, Mr. Houston. In seeking a relationship with the Lord, God doesn't require that we have a mediator save Jesus Christ Himself. Countless people have come to know Him in a one-on-one conversion. If you are able to establish that relationship apart from our assistance, we'll rejoice with you. If you don't need our help, well and good. I have no desire to wade though sinful pollution with anybody. I have enough of my own dirty linens to keep cleaned up."

Cody's expression changed. He looked shocked and a bit shameful as he said, "I hear what you're saying. I, uh, I have attempted to do just that but I don't think I know how to say what He wants to hear. I don't get anywhere."

"Then," quipped Kyle, "I would say you need help—that is, if you want to be counted among the redeemed children of God. You want redemption? Are you satisfied with your lost condition?

"Lost?" He was indignant. "Are you saying I'm lost?"

"Let's put it this way: do you have sins you've never confessed or can't admit, even to God? If so, I would say you're not in a relationship, and if that relationship is missing, then you're lost."

Cody was visibly shaken, and Weeda noticed he was taking on the same miserable expression she had seen in her office the day he pleaded for help. His response was, "Well, I-I-I can't bring myself to talk about some things."

"Not even to God?"

"Not even to God."

"Then," said Kyle, "today's your opportunity to get those things out and have them covered by the Blood of Jesus."

At the mention of the Blood, Cody gasped and looked as though he was going to be sick, and with a tremor in his voice, "So then, where do I start?"

"You must confess those sins which you've been unable to talk about."

He finally pierced his response toward them with eyes that were as hard as steel. "Do I have your word that my confession will be confidential?"

"That's fully explained on the cover page of the forms you have in your hands. We'll need to see those to get started." Slowly Cody handed them over.

Kyle looked over the papers, and in his professional manner briefly commented on or discussed some of the answered questions which, in summary, revealed that Cody had been reared by parents who by community standards were wealthy landowners, having inherited extensive acreage from Cody's grandfather. The family had cultivated cotton, which for many years brought in a fortune, but with the invasion of the boll weevil, that lucrative industry petered out. With cotton no longer king, they turned to raising and buying timber and selling lumber—a business Cody had continued after his father's death. Kyle readily detected that they had been people users and asked the question: "Did you father take advantage of his workers, especially those who worked on shares?"

"Well, I don't know—probably. I didn't see it that way while I was growing up, but now, looking back, I see things a little differently."

"So his practices didn't bother you then? Would such dealings bother you now?"

"I'll have to think about that. Offhand, I'd say yes and no. Some things would; some things wouldn't. I mean, I suppose at times and in some things he was unfair, but there has to be some compensation for taking the responsibility for those who won't exactly take responsibility for themselves. He benefited them, so it was only fair that he should be benefited in return."

"So today you have expanded the timber and lumber business. You've incorporated several other endeavors into Houston Enterprises?"

"Right."

"Do you have that same attitude toward your workers?"

"Well, you almost have to retain some of that mentality. It takes a lot of capital, a lot of time, and a lot of energy to keep such an enterprise productive, and I feel I'm entitled to the...how shall I say it without sounding, uh, prideful?"

"Respect and standing?"

"Of course! But labor-wise, things are so different for me than they were for my father. He was able to make decisions about his workers that I'm not free to make. The government makes them for me."

"Are you saying the only thing that keeps you from using your workers to their disadvantage are governmental regulations?"

"I'm not sure I can answer that. I just don't know."

"We'll move on. From what I see, I'm assuming you had a good relationship with your parents?"

"I did."

"Being an only child, you were probably spared the stress that arises in families with several children—rivalries, jealousies, competition, and the like?"

"I think that's a reasonable conclusion."

"But on the other hand, were there downsides to being an only child that you need to talk about?"

"I don't think so. I had an active life with a minimum of loneliness, I'd say."

"And you were an average student through high school and a good student at Tulane? Success in that also?"

"Average, I suppose. Some thought I had too much social life. I didn't think so."

"Any cheating?"

"Some, but very little, comparatively speaking."

"Then you'll need to repent of that."

"But everybody did it."

"Mr. Houston, Christians are not everybody. They are a special people, called out to be peculiar for the cause of Christ. When dealing with the Lord, the Scriptures speak directly to each person on an individual basis and when it comes to getting right with God, the norm is irrelevant."

"Well, I, uh, never heard it put just that way."

"And those romantic involvements you've listed—where sex was a part, you must seek the Lord's forgiveness."

"But I never forced myself on anybody. Where there was sex, it was the result of mutual consent."

"Mutual consent? That's not God's criterion for making judgments. Having the partner's consent is one thing; having God's approval is another matter. You had your partner's OK but that's not synonymous with God's OK. You violated those women, and you need to seek forgiveness for those violations."

"But everybody—I mean many Christians do those things. I'm confused, really confused." After a long pause, he found some words. "Dr. Sanders, tell me. How does anybody make it to heaven?"

"I'm glad you asked that. The answer is grace—grace provided through the sacrificial death of God's Son. You are not meeting the requirements for this gift of grace, and until you do, you'll have no relationship with Jesus Christ, and you'll miss out on God's plan of salvation. Cheating and fornication are abominations to God, but those misdeeds won't keep you out of heaven once they are confessed and put under the blood of Jesus Christ. The monumental sin you're guilty of is your failure to confess and accept his forgiveness for having committed them. I want to reiterate: if you miss heaven, it won't be because you engaged in immoral acts, as heinous as those things are, but because you failed to bring these sins to God through confession and ask for his forgiveness. When dealing with God, you must deal with him on his terms, using his definitions pertaining to sin, to redemption, to forgiveness, to justification, and to every other provision that makes up our salvation package. One must call a spade a spade and accept God's views as to what constitutes sin. God's labels matter; yours and mine don't count. That's the reason cultural norms—the 'everybody's doing it' excuse—carry no weight in the prayer closet. It's imperative that we know the Scriptures so we can concur with him in his definitions and hold his views concerning Himself, the world, and all things therein. It's important that we know what He has to say about mankind, about angels, about devils, and accept the absolutes he has spelled out. You are offending God when you value your own opinions to the extent that those opinions determine the manner in which you regard him and attempt to approach him. Am I coming through?"

"Certainly, certainly, certainly. I don't know what to say. I never heard anybody talk like this. I am at a loss. As I say, I'm at a loss as to what to do first. I've never heard these things. Do preachers know these things?"

"A good question, but one we won't have time to deal with here. You've no doubt been exposed to these teachings, but because you were prideful in holding your own viewpoints, Satan deafened your ears and blinded your eyes to these truths. He has the power to do that if we lack humility concerning the things of God. Before we go further, we need to pray. I'll lead, then it'll be your turn to talk to the Father."

"I hear what you're saying, but you see, that's where I'm hung up."

"Then that's where we'll start. After I've prayed, you just tell the Lord why you're here. Start with the problem, which, according to what you've told Weeda and me, is your inability to pray and make contact. That problem is not unique to you. Satan knows that success with God hinges on one's ability to talk with Him, agree with Him by confessing who He claims to be as recorded in His Word. The devil doesn't want you to get past that hurdle, because agreeing with God concerning the birth, death, and resurrection of Jesus Christ puts you on the road to success. When you make these confessions from the heart, then you're ready to do business with God. You're a businessman, Mr. Houston, and I'm sure your clients and customers have to deal with you on your terms. Could you expect God to do less? Now that we've established that fact, let's go back to one of the greatest privileges available to man—that of prayer. I'll lead, then you follow." Kyle prayed.

"Dear God, we praise You and thank You for having revealed to us who You are. You've made that revelation through Your written Word, the Holy Bible. You've spoken through the Patriarchs, through Your prophets, through Your son, and through His chosen disciples. Weeda and I are grateful you have enabled us through the work of the Holy Spirit to receive these truths into our hearts. We've learned that confessing these truths enables us to do business with You. In this business process, we have received forgiveness for our sins because we've been obedient to confess our sins to You. We are redeemed and have the assurance of that redemption because we have followed Your prescribed remedy as outlined in Your Word.

"Now, Lord, we bring Cody to You. He is seeking a personal relationship with Jesus and wants to experience the redemption that such a relationship provides. So we are here to assist him in this endeavor; therefore, in the powerful name of Jesus, we break down the barriers that Satan has erected in his mind against the knowledge of Your word, and we bring to naught all those things that hinder or prevent this man's salvation. We tear down the strongholds that have blinded him—all those things which have deafened him to the true gospel. We destroy pride and fear and any other intellectual or emotional attitudes that would interfere with his being able to pray and talk to You personally. By faith we make this petition. Amen."

When Kyle opened his eyes, Cody was resting his head on the desk, using his folded arms as a cushion. At first, there was no response, just silence. Then suddenly, Cody groaned, an anguished moan, and started sobbing convulsively. Kyle and Weeda exchanged nods, indicating they were pleased with what was happening. They felt confident the Holy Spirit had begun His redemptive work, and they respectfully allowed Him all the time he needed to bring conviction. They continued to pray silently.

After several minutes, Cody quieted down, looked up, and apologized. "I'm sorry. I don't know what happened, but something did."

"Don't apologize, just be grateful something is happening. Are you ready to pray?"

Looking at them with longing eyes, he answered. "I'll try. I hope I can. I need relief. You have no idea how I'm hurting. I mean—not physically, but I'm in pain. Please help me."

"Mr. Houston, at this stage, take your eyes off us and call out to God."

Without further ado, Cody cried out. "God, I'm so sorry I've lived a lie—a lie, Lord, before my family, in the community, in the church. I'm so ashamed. How can I get things straightened out? If You'll show me, I'll try, but You know how things are tangled up. How can I risk people finding out? How can I keep going on? How? How? How can I function? People have regarded me with respect, but I've just found out that You see me as vile and repulsive. I am a wretched sinner in need of Your help. I'll do anything You say. I give up, Lord, I give up. I give myself to You. I don't know what You can do with me or why You would want me, but I'm Yours. Just give me some relief and peace."

He became quiet and rested his head on the table again. His silence was broken only with long sighs now and then. When he finally looked up, his expression was a mixture of both relief and sadness as he stuttered, "I-I-I don't-don't know how to say this, but I think I'll have to make my confessions to you. Tell me that's not necessary, that I can make my confessions silently to God. Please tell me that."

"I can't tell you that, Mr. Houston, because the Holy Spirit who imparted that knowledge to you has also revealed the same thing to me, and Weeda is nodding her head indicating that she's getting the same impression. I can appreciate your desire to deal privately with God. I'm unable to explain why God sometimes requires open and public confessions, but there are times when He does. I think I heard you tell the Lord that you are willing to do whatever He exacts. Were you sincere in making that offer?"

"Yes, Dr. Sanders. I have to have some peace I just thought, maybe..."

"Don't you recall? When you do business with God, you do it on His terms. Sounds as though He's sounding out His terms."

"Oh, I don't know how I can, but I'm afraid not to. I don't want God to give up on me now."

"Rest assured, He won't, but you do have to cooperate on His terms. We'll help you."

"And you promised confidentiality?" To which they signaled a "yes."

"I'm sorry. I feel kinda sick. I'd like some water. Where's the fountain?"

Weeda spoke up. "It's right outside the door, but I'll get you some, unless you need to walk around."

"Thank you. I just need some water," and Weeda was back in a jiffy with a tumbler full. He began sipping slowly, which Kyle interpreted as a delay tactic, putting off as long as possible the dreaded confession. But he would not be sidetracked. The man's spiritual freedom hinged on coming clean.

"So, Mr. Houston, what are these misdeeds you need to confess?"

"Well, you've already pointed out cheating and immorality."

"Yes. You've freely admitted to those, so just tell God that you're sorry you've used people to your advantage and that you've violated His laws of morality, being sure to name each partner. Call each woman by her first name. We don't know who you're referring to but God does. Express your sorrow for the times you've cheated for academic reasons or for economic advantage. OK?"

Cody bowed his head and prayed according to what Kyle had specified and asked for God's forgiveness. After he finished, Kyle assured him that God's forgiveness had been granted because he had prayed according to God's prescribed remedy.

Cody demonstrated a tinge of gratitude by nodding his head while exhaling a long sigh—breath that seemingly had been pent up much too long. Kyle watched him closely as the sighs continued, waiting to see if he would come forth with additional confessions without further prodding—which he didn't, so Kyle took the initiative.

"Now, you need to deal with those misdeeds you've been unable to discuss, not even with God. When you confess, you won't be telling God something He doesn't already know. You'll just be admitting, agreeing with Him that those misdeeds were sinful and that you're sorry for having committed them."

"Yes, yes, yes, I'm beginning to understand."

"From these forms, I note that your greatest disappointment was learning that your wife could not have children. Were you angry with God?"

"How did you know? To tell the truth, I'm still angry at times. Much of what you and Ms. McVey would consider sinful in my life came about because we could not have children of our own—at least Anna couldn't, and no way could you begin to understand how important that is to a man who has heard all his life that the family property must remain under the family name. I was made to believe it was my duty to keep the Houston possessions and the family name intact. Much of what I did can be chalked up to that feeling of obligation."

Both Weeda and Kyle were sympathetically moved, but Kyle was hanging tough. "Whatever it was you did and regardless of the pressures, you won't get relief and find peace until you have made the necessary confessions. God is aware of your struggles, but that aside, still you are required to deal with sin on His terms. Remember?"

"I'm beginning to, Dr. Sanders. I'm beginning to." At this point, Weeda was uptight but hoping it wasn't noticeable. She was so glad Kyle was in the lead. He looked as relaxed as a Raggedy Ann doll. She wondered what his next probe would be, and then it came.

"I believe the Lord would have you relay the details of the adoption."

"That's the hardest part. You see, I did something which, so far as I know, only one woman and I have ever had any knowledge."

"And what is this deed that you and this woman have managed to keep secret from everybody but God?"

Cody took a deep breath, looked down for a few seconds then lifted his head, saying, "Anna and I wanted a child, but Anna was unable to conceive, so we decided to adopt. Since I was fertile, something in me wouldn't let me deny myself fatherhood. I wanted my own biological offspring, so I made arrangements to impregnate another woman with the understanding that after the delivery, Anna and I could adopt the child but keep forever concealed the true identity of the biological parents."

Weeda had been holding her breath but at that point she exhaled to the extent that Kyle gave her foot a nudge, conveying a "keep calm" message, but to Cody he said, "That must have required some detailed arrangements with a great deal of micro-management thrown in. Were you romantically attached to the child's mother?"

"Not so much at the time of conception, but later it was or has been very hard to stay detached."

"Are you telling me the biological mother didn't get out of the picture after the adoption was legalized?"

"No, she didn't," and after some delay, he added, "you see, Sonny's mother is my secretary, Ms. Sheldon."

Weeda was stunned and inadvertently butted in. "And the people here in Rushton didn't know about her pregnancy?"

"No, we arranged for her to go to California for several months on the pretense of nursing and caring for a much-loved relative, an aunt to be precise. After the reported demise of the aunt, she returned to Rushton and to her former job as my executive secretary. Upon her return, she feigned a delightful surprise that Anna and I had succeeded in adopting a fine baby boy. Since Anna was active in so many church and civic affairs, she was always grateful for Ms. Sheldon's assistance in caring for Sonny. When we were away on weekends, we could always count on her to keep Sonny in her home."

"Certainly that must have been hard on Ms. Sheldon—having to deny her true identity to her son all these years?"

"I know it has been, but that was the agreement, and she's lived up to it."

"It's hard to believe she could hide her true feelings—that people didn't detect something unusual or special about the relationship."

"But you'd have to understand the situation. Everybody loved Sonny. He was everybody's child. Family and friends were partial to the boy. For that reason, her attention and affections didn't stand out."

"Anna never had an inkling?"

"None that was ever noticeable. You'd have to know her to understand. She's a trusting person and thinks people, if they haven't been convicted of a crime and placed behind bars, are just like her, incapable of wrong doing. You might say she's a 'Gone with-the-wind' Melanie."

"Amazing! These days so many of us are critics and faultfinders." Looking down at the forms, Kyle posed another lead-in question. "Let's see. Sonny is what age? About eighteen. Have you through the years never been fearful that the cover on this clandestine deal would get blown off?"

"No, not really. How could it unless one of us talked?"

"But you had to legalize the adoption. Surely there was an agency involved?"

"Dr. Sanders, there are ways to work around most anything."

"I suppose so. Is it possible that Ms. Sheldon has talked?"

At this juncture, Weeda was tempted to violate Sonny's confidence and tell how Sonny had come to question his birth lineage, but instinctively she knew that by doing so she'd lose out as his confidante, and her prime responsibility as a school counselor was the student. Instead, she asked, "What about Sonny's feelings for Ms. Sheldon?"

"He has high regard for her and is appreciative of all she's done. He seems to have viewed her special care of him as a service to the family, just as he considers her loyalty to the business as commendable."

"In some previous comments, you indicated that your actions and reactions toward Ms. Sheldon have been difficult at times. Does that mean you two have been sexually active?"

"A few times, now and then, but I never neglected Anna."

Kyle couldn't refrain: "Maybe that's because she's a Melanie who, if you remember, never suspected anything between Ashley and Scarlet."

Cody shrugged his shoulders as if to say he wasn't concerned about the whys of her acceptance so long as the acceptance remained intact.

Kyle kept probing, seeking some way to bring conviction. "Lately, you've expressed some remorse for this double life—for instance, as you prayed just now. When did this remorse set in?"

Cody took his time to ponder the question, then slowly answered. "At the time I had that second conference with Ms. McVey. Until that day, I'd never given much thought to it. I mean, I wasn't seeing anything wrong in it."

"Just a minute! If you felt OK about what you had done and were still doing, why did you think it necessary to keep it concealed? Why did you hide it? If in your mind it was legal and moral, why did you go to such lengths to keep it secretive?"

"Well, the way I felt about it was not the way society would have viewed it, had they known about it. They would have rejected both me and Sally Sheldon. But I see things differently. I've always felt that unless my actions bring harm to someone else, then what I do is my business. So far I've never seen that what I did harmed anybody. In fact, I've seen good in the situation: a childless couple was no longer childless; my obligation to keep the family's name and the property intact was met, and Sally's security for life was guaranteed."

"That's the way you have rationalized it all these years so you've been comfortable in your deception, but let me say again that if you're going to get right with God, you have to look at your actions from His perspective. I hope that truth is beginning to sink into your spirit."

"I'm seeing that and I'm learning that, and that's what's so painful. I do get some relief every time I make a confession. Does that mean I need to be more specific in my confessions?"

"I would say so. Look at your misdeeds from God's point of view. Who was violated? Who was betrayed? Who was encouraged to sin with you? Who besides yourself was required to live a lie?"

"Oh me, oh my!" And at that point he started praying without being told. "God, I'm sorry for my immoral conduct with Sally Sheldon—for the arrangement we made, for causing her to sin with me, for betraying Anna's trust. I'm sorry I've lived a lie all these years." He ceased praying but continued weeping, and his shoulders shook under the weight of such emotional distress. When the shaking subsided, he resumed his praying.

"Lord, I don't see how You can grant it, but I'm asking Your forgiveness. Please forgive me and help me. Oh how I need Your help! I've always known how to fix things, but I have not the slightest idea about how to fix this predicament. I love Sonny, how I love that boy, and I love Anna, and I love Sally, Sonny's mother. How can I bear this coming to light? Will it have to be revealed for the entire world to see? I know I'm getting right with You. I can feel it, but how do I make things right with Sonny and with Anna? And there's Sally. Will she forgive me for breaking my promise to secrecy? I've never had to admit my mistakes to anyone. I've always expected people to accept me, right or wrong, and they have. I've never had any practice in apologizing, and it's hard for people my age to start doing things differently. I'll study Your Word and try to learn what true Christianity is all about. Am I making sense, Lord?"

With that question, he became quiet and lowered his head on the desk. Kyle and Weeda sat quietly, scribbling on their notepads. Kyle was pondering about his next move when Cody lifted his head and with a settled look, took the lead. "I'm open to advice. You heard my prayer. You know my predicament. Do you have any advice?"

"None, except to say that I heard you ask God for His advice and direction, so I think wisdom dictates that you wait on the Lord and give Him time to answer that prayer. He is always faithful. Give Him the opportunity to show that faithfulness. Incidentally, how are you feeling?"

"I can't explain it. Being able to make contact with God tops anything I've ever experienced. For two weeks I've tried to talk to Him, but I couldn't even find words. I had given up. Believe you me, it's a desperate place to be when you know there's a God but you don't have access to Him."

"I would think so."

"So now, based on what I've done and what I'm feeling, I think I've been born again."

Almost in unison, they both agreed and gave praise and thanksgiving to the Lord to which Kyle added: "Why don't we close this session with prayer and wait on the Lord about any further steps?"

"Yes, yes. I don't know what lies ahead, but I do know that the greatest hurdle, making contact with God, has been overcome." Kyle prayed a closing prayer after which they both saw Cody to the door. Before departing, he turned and embraced them with a hug that spoke meanings into their hearts that words could not convey. Cody Houston had found a measure of freedom and eternal salvation for his soul.

* * *

On Saturday evening at Westwinds, Kyle and Weeda pampered their taste buds with one of their favorite meals—fresh grilled tuna, saffron rice, and a medley of fresh vegetables. While they were sharing their thoughts about the news and personal matters, Weeda brought up the subject of Kyle's parents.

"Kyle, I enjoyed being with your mother and dad the other evening. You're so much like your mother, even your mannerisms and speech patterns."

"That's what people say. She's quite a woman, so I always feel complimented when people liken me to her. They had some nice things to say about you, to which I naturally agreed, of course."

"Gee thanks. I suppose you can tell my mother is fond of you, and I hope you can meet my brother the next time he visits in these parts. I still find myself wishing I had a father you could meet."

"I understand, but you are coming to terms with your feelings about him, aren't you?"

"Thanks to you and the Corleys, yes. It's not on my mind nearly so much, and I'm not bitter. I'm convinced it was the bitterness that kept me churning. The sadness would come and go, but the bitterness had taken up residence and never let up—that is, not until that day in Dellisville."

"What about the fear?"

"I can't really assess that," but after some deliberation, she added, "I think maybe the suspicion that every man deviates to some degree in his sexuality has lessened. That suspicion made me feel vulnerable, and coming to know you has also helped to offset that mentality."

"Tell me, did you have suspicions about me in the beginning?"

"Consciously, I really don't know, but unconsciously, I probably did. I'm afraid I didn't trust your motives."

"That's an honest answer. I asked that question partly because, as a physician, it's important that I come across as a person with honorable intentions."

"I'm sure you do. As you well know, I had hang-ups not common to most women. At least, I hope the majority of women are not in that kind of bondage,"

"Aren't you glad you went to Dellisville?"

"Am I ever? In fact, I'd like another session with the Corleys as soon as I get out from under this Houston case."

"Good, that can be arranged. Speaking of the Houstons, any new developments?"

"I'm not aware of anything, but Macy did tell me she broke off her friendship with Sonny."

"Because of what is going on?"

"Yes, that plus the fact that her parents insisted upon it. Sonny's behavior is still spiraling downward, I understand. Seems everybody's aware that he's off track—a different person."

"The changes are that noticeable?"

"Very obvious, I'm told. As his father told us, he is seen as preoccupied, sulky, inattentive, depressed."

"Sounds suspiciously like drugs."

"That's what Macy thinks. He has chosen to avoid me except for that one time when he called me late at night asking for prayer—said he was in a tight spot, trapped, and needed help. He had to cut the call short for some reason, as though he was being watched." She slowed down and then continued. "I earnestly prayed for his safety and release. He asked me to keep the call confidential, which I did, but I was determined to seek help and get others involved had he not showed up for school the next morning, which he did, so I relaxed on that score; but after class when I tried to get his attention in the hallway, he ignored my effort and avoided me. I offered him some counseling time through issued passes but he never showed up. At the request of teachers, Mr. Drago summoned him to his office but didn't get anywhere. Since the boy had not really violated any school rules, Drago's pitch centered on his academic slump. Drago later attempted to arrange a three-way conference with Sonny and his parents, but that effort didn't go over with Cody, and you can guess the reason."

"He's afraid of what might come to light."

"Of course. So far as I know, Drago and the faculty members have no knowledge of the basic problem."

"But the lid is bound to come off sooner or later."

"Hopefully, it won't be through me."

"I'm with you on that. You've asked God to work in your behalf so trust him to do just that. We'll look on the bright side, remembering that one good thing has already emerged. Cody has come to know the Lord and has promised the Lord that he is willing to do anything that He requires, so in a sense, what comes next is between Cody and the Lord. Whatever else surfaces now that Cody is redeemed is bonus. I've been praying that Sonny will experience a breakthrough, though I can't be specific since I don't know precisely what his problem is. I can just imagine he's going around wondering just who he is, fearing he's not who he thought he was. Cody is scheduled to see us again next Saturday. Right?"

"Yes, and I have mixed emotions about it. I'm looking forward to any good that will come but somehow dreading that something might backfire."

"We'll cross that bridge Saturday. On the phone this morning you said you had a report about the Bible study."

"Oh yes. Macy says she has, or at least her mother has, the names of more than fifty students who have registered."

"Good! Are you getting ready to teach?"

"Kyle, you know and I know that you're supposed to teach that study, so that's settled. OK?"

"How can you be so certain?"

"Because I've been praying, asking the Lord to identify the teacher, and I don't get a peace about any other person but you."

"I must say I'm not elated over the thought of taking on another responsibility, but I am pleased that you came to such a definite conclusion through the avenue of prayer. Being able to reach conclusion and make decisions through prayer is an indication of your Christian growth."

Weeda stopped eating and leveled her gaze at him. "Is that statement to me personally or is it a comment that you would make to any other Christian?"

"Both. I rejoice in the growth of all Christians, but I'm especially interested in your growth."

"I suppose I'm supposed to ask why?"

"And I suppose I'm supposed to explain?"

"Only if you want. I'd like to hear your reason, but I won't press for it."

"You don't need to, and I don't think an explanation is necessary. You know full well why I'm interested in your spiritual growth: for the same reason I'm interested in my own. For me a permanent relationship, though desirable, is not absolutely essential. I would like the stability that such a bond would afford. I'd treasure the intimacy, the sharing and all that, but there are things more important to me than any earthly relationship. I hope you know me well enough to accept what I'm saying without taking offense. I wouldn't want to consider committing to someone who isn't of the same mind frame."

Laying down her fork, she stopped eating and on the verge of tears, blurted our, "Kyle, is this a proposal?"

"My dear, this is hardly the place for that. Let's just say this is a testing of the waters."

"Are you saying that your coming forth with a proposal hinges on my Christian growth?"

"Well, I suppose you might take it that way."

"Kyle, that's saying you don't accept me as I am. That hurts."

"It shouldn't. After what you went through with Lanny, you should be grateful that my interest in you extends beyond the social and physical. Men the world over establish relationships with women for the sole purpose of enjoying them physically and social-ly with never a thought given to their spiritual welfare. I don't think I want to be guilty of that."

"When you put it that way, Kyle, I'm so touched. I don't think I can eat anything else."

"Oh, yes you can. We'll change the subject."

"I don't want to change the subject. I like what you're saying."

Kyle was enjoying the reaction he was getting and reached across the table, giving her hand a squeeze and saying, "Let's finish our tuna steaks before they get cold, and while we're finishing up, I want to request your prayers for one of my patients."

Weeda's eyes were so glazed over by the emotion of the moment that she had difficult responding, "Will you say that again, about the prayer?" And after his restatement, she answered: "Sure, of course. Turn about is fair play. You've been a prayer warrior in my behalf. I'm more than glad you're asking. Who and what?"

"It's for a lady. I'll just call her Lola. She's a professing Christian, and I emphasize 'professing.' She's a church member, the mother of two lovely children. Until recently she was happily married. She's still married, but not happily. In fact, she's miserable, coming apart at the seams, coming unglued."

"How sad. What happened?"

"An abortion. A few months ago, by choice, she destroyed a seven-week fetus and now she's the victim of what I call PAD—Post Abortion Depression."

"How do explain the syndrome—this PAD? I mean from a physician's perspective."

"From a physician's perspective, I stick to observations and anec-dotal records which show that a high percentage of women who abort their babies come down with some form of neurosis. I would estimate about eighty percent. That's a medical viewpoint. From a Christian perspective, I have concluded that the malady has a spiri-tual base."

"Sadly interesting, and knowing you, I'm sure it'll be easy to prove your point."

"Understanding the why is really not complicated. It's like the other sins we've discussed from time to time. It needs to be con-fessed as sin and dealt with accordingly. Many women have been brainwashed to believe that a fetus is just a blob of tissue that can be discarded without compunction. That's the world's view, the mentality of the deceived, but just because the mind accepts a lie doesn't necessarily mean the human spirit concedes." He detected question marks in Weeda's expression, so he paused.

"Sorry, I got off track. The part about the mind and the spirit— say that again."

"Sorry! I was saying that many women accept the lie that abortion is a sinless act and when confronted by the critics, use various rationales to justify their actions. According to the writer of Hebrews, God has written his laws in our hearts, which means that the human spirit knows the truth—that abortion is the destruction of human life. I need to abbreviate so we can vacate this table, so I'll make it fast.

"As I was saying, the spirit, having been imprinted with God's laws, rejects the lie which the mind has accepted, so a battle takes place between the deceived mind and the informed spirit. Both are battling for the soul's compliance. Paul, in the sixth and seventh chapters of Romans, pens some graphic statements about this kind of internal warfare. Such conflicts often engender personality pathologies such as Lola is now suffering. One of the works of the Holy Spirit is to convict believers of their wrongdoings. I don't know how long such wrestling goes on. I suppose it differs from person to person, but I should think that after a time God ceases to struggle with recalcitrant people."

"Such sobering thoughts, not only where abortions are concerned but any other unconfessed sins. The way you put it, this puts guilt in a positive light, as a catalyst God uses to bring people to repentance. I was taught to regard it as a negative, the enemy of self-esteem and self worth, the breeding ground for insecurity."

"Guilt can be a negative but not if it originates with the Holy Spirit. The guilt trip He imposes should be respected as God's correction. Otherwise, the unconfessed sin can bring on severe neurotic symptoms."

"That's the positive side. Now what about the negative side? You most have some thoughts on that?"

"Logical deductions, my dear, and to carry the reasoning further is to equate the negative with God's enemy, the devil."

"I can follow that reasoning OK, but what I want to know: how do you tell the difference? How do you determine the source of your guilt? That's kinda scary."

"It's not always easy. Some people have a gift for determining such things, but for those who are not so gifted, prayer is the recourse. There are a few general guidelines that can help. Guilt having its source in God is usually specific and can be pinpointed—the kind of guilt the prophet Nathan laid on David, which led him to repentance after he had sinned with Bathsheba. Guilt imposed from the devil is usually vague, generalized, and comes as accusations dealing mainly with sins of omission rather than sins of commission. For instance, Lola's sin is one of commission."

"That's sobering. I've never heard much about this from the pulpit."

"So true. We don't hear condemnation of sin. No warnings against adultery, bribery, extortion, and the like. Much of the preaching is put to the tune of a social gospel, carrying very little convicting power. These social messages chastise church members for what they fail to do. They haven's visited the sick; they haven't supported the church programs; they haven't tithed—on and on. If preachers could succeed in getting people to confess and repent of their committed sins, then the sins of omission would become almost non items because the people could then be guided by the Holy Spirit to carry out their Christian duties as outlined by the gospel writers. People who have a right relationship with God don't have to be reminded to tithe, to pray, to minister. Doing those things become as innate to the truly redeemed as the warble is to the warbler. A bird can't help singing. It's in his nature, and so it is with those who have no unconfessed sin between themselves and God. They naturally behave like who they are, children of God, and they don't have to be begged into doing so. They are like the warbler who warbles because it's structured into his DNA. Back to King David: After he confessed his sin of commission, he automatically got his priorities lined up, and his sins of omission were a thing of the past. He started behaving as a child of God."

"Yes, I think I can see that, but I want to go back to what you were talking about before—about determining the source of guilt. If, after seeking God through prayer, one doesn't get clues as to the source, than what?"

"He should be suspicious that the devil is the source of the condemnation and deal with him. The book of James gives some good advice—submitting and humbling oneself unto God causes the devil to flee and carry his accusations with him."

"Those things you're saying lead me to ponder about some of the counseling principles I've been taught."

"I can understand. Many professional therapists view all guilt as totally negative—a mental and emotional state to be eliminated, baggage to be discarded. Some of it is just that, but there are times when guilt is to the soul what pain is to the body, a signal that something has gone haywire and needs to be fixed. Whatever the source, guilt deserves attention. The prescribed remedy for getting relief hinges, as I said, on the source."

"I'm thinking I need to see the Corleys again."

"Knowledge of the truth dragging up something, eh?"

"Possibly."

"After we've seen the Houstons on Saturday, I'll make the arrangements; they expect to do some follow-up with you."

"Thanks. There's something I want to mention, about you personally."

"Sure, shoot."

"When you were selling me on the idea of going for counseling, you mentioned that you yourself had benefited from the process. I can't imagine that you ever had a need for it. I'm not putting you on a pedestal outside the realm of ordinary human experiences and weaknesses, but I can't believe you ever had any maladjustments that needed that kind of attention."

Kyle laughed heartily and long. "You didn't know me in my 'BC' days, before I came to know Christ; however, you are partially right. I don't think I had any hang-ups that hampered me mentally or socially, but I surely had some sins to confess. Fortunately, the Lord started dealing with me when I was in college, and I'm so grateful I had the good sense to respond and submit. I still wrestle, wobble, and miss the mark. I'll tell you more about it later. After all, I insisted on knowing some of your background, and I do hope you don't think my insistence was just a selfish curiosity. I detected you needed help. I hope you believe that."

"Indeed I do, and I'm grateful."

"Now back to Lola. When we get to your place, I'd like you to join me in prayer in her behalf. Right now her eyes are blinded by the enemy. It'll take the power of the Holy Spirit to make her receptive to the truth concerning the basis of her problem and the neurosis. The opportunity to help could be lost if I should get over zealous. In fact, my assignment is to pray for her, and the Lord may use someone else to deal with her spiritually, or He may choose to give her a one-on-one experience as He gave Paul on the Damascus Road. He is so filled with infinite variety in the ways He relates to us sinners and saints. Remember how He made the analogy? 'You never know from whence the wind comes nor where it will blow.' For believers this uncertainty of how He will do a thing, enclosed by the certainty that He will, makes for some high adventure in the Christian walk, and I think that not knowing the 'how' tends to keep us humble. We can't put God in a box."

"To say the least."

"I see our server looking in this direction. He looks as though he's ready for us to vamoose." They quickly departed.

After some prayer time at her place, Kyle left for home, and Weeda was disappointed that she had failed to bring up the subject of his 'BC' days. Sometimes, he just plainly irritated her by exercising more emotional control than was normal for any human being, especially for a man. In the beginning, he had seen the same thing in her, but her rigid control was a by-product of fear, and that should be understandable. She didn't believe Kyle was afraid of anything—internally or externally. What would be his explanation if she should ask? She just might get up the courage to do so.

* * *

Saturday afternoon Cody waited outside the Triplex Medical Center for at least thirty minutes before Kyle and Weeda arrived. "Whew!" sighed Cody as they walked to Kyle's office together, "I was afraid you were standing me up."

Kyle shook his head. "No way. Traffic held us up. There's been an accident at the intersection of Principal and Forest."

"I heard the sirens. No injuries, I hope."

"We couldn't tell. We were backed up a couple of blocks, then the cops rerouted us, so we were never that close."

Kyle unlocked his office, and they took their places as before, Cody seated across the desk from Weeda and Kyle. He seemed keyed up and ready to get started. To refresh their memories and to facilitate dialogue, Kyle read aloud portions of his notes from the previous session which had ended with Cody's asking the Lord to guide him in his efforts to make things right with Anna, with Sally, and with Sonny. Then laying his notes aside, he said, "That was a timely and wise request you made of the Lord, Mr. Houston."

"Thanks to you! You encouraged me to pray that way. Good counsel. In fact, that's the reason I'm back. I want you two to pray with me. I need some more Godly guidance."

"Hopefully, we can provide it. That's why we're here. It's good to see you on such a positive note. Feel free to share what's going on."

"Well, I haven't made any direct efforts to get things squared away with Anna or Sonny yet, though that was foremost in my mind when I left here that day. But I have made progress with Sally, and I have a report that's unbelievable."

"Sounds as though you and God have been busy. In what way?"

"What's come about may not line up with what you might have expected. You see, I haven't confessed to Sally that I broke my vow by sharing the adoption secret. That will come later. I'm still confessing and getting things right. Something else happened that more or less put that one thing on the back burner."

"We're listening", said Weeda. "Keep talking."

"What I'm about to tell you happened just a few days ago. It was late in the afternoon, and everybody had left from the office except the two of us. I was at my desk praying, trying to figure out a way to make my confession to her when she knocked. When she walked in, she had the most puzzling look on her face, so I asked if something was wrong. She said she had come in to ask me something along the same line. Said she had noticed a change in my behavior and in my countenance and wondered what was going on with me." Placing his hand over his heart, he continued, "I was shocked but glad that the change so evident to me from within was noticeable to others from the outside."

"God gave you an opportunity to share, and I'm sensing you did just that."

"You're right, and I was surprised at how honest I could be with her about it. Since you two are not financial or business counselors, she was surprised that I was seeking help from you but understood when I explained how our recent problems with Sonny had led me to seek counsel from his school counselor. That really got her attention because she has been very upset about Sonny.

"Anyway, I told her what had happened to me—that I'd been born again. Would you believe she accepted what I told her without question, saying she wanted the same thing for herself?"

Weeda couldn't refrain. "Are you telling us you brought her to the Lord?"

"That's exactly what happened."

"Sounds as though you're one of those born-agains who might be contagious!"

"Well, no offense, doctor, but if that's the case, I don't think I'll seek treatment for it."

"I heard that. Did you get down to the nitty-gritty?'"

"I tried to. Using those scripture passages you had given me, I answered her questions as best I could. We must have spent two hours poring over a small Bible I purchased after I left here that day. I tried my best to deal with her the same way you had dealt with me. I told her if she wanted a personal relationship with the Lord she had to come to a place of Godly sorrow about the sins she had committed, and she did just that. She confessed and sought forgiveness for things I had no idea she was guilty of, and it brought results."

"Did she deal with her betrayal of Anna's trust?"

"She did. In fact, we both did, but we're still praying about how we're going to inform her about Sonny's birth. I can't explain it, but I believe the Lord is going to work it out—set up circumstances so we can get all these dastardly things under the redeeming Blood of Christ."

"How amazing!" said Weeda. And Kyle added his praises and thanksgiving.

Cody was still bubbling over. "And do you know, Sally wants to schedule a counseling session with you as soon as you can arrange to see her—says she's reading the Bible until midnight every night. She's read through Matthew, John, Romans, and Hebrews since her conversion. Says she can't put the Book down when she's awake."

"That's how the Holy Spirit works. It'll be interesting to see how God intervenes in the midst of these entanglements."

Cody nodded his head. "You know, I dread confronting Anna and Sonny with what I've done, but what has happened so far makes me believe God will come through in some miraculous way, so the dread gets put down by the hope. Does that make sense?"

"Sure," said Kyle. "That's faith at work. Faith is a gift, a mysterious power I can't explain, but I know both from the Bible and from personal experience that it's a powerful force. The dynamics of it only God understands. I like to think of it as the raw material God uses to answer our prayers."

Cody butted in: "I've been praying night and day for Sonny, and I've come to the place that what people think about what I've done is not what's driving me. I don't mean I don't care what they think, because I do. In fact, I'm deeply ashamed, but what's important to me now is getting Sonny straightened out. Anna knows the Lord, and no doubt it has been her prayers that have brought me to the place I am today."

"So true," said Kyle "and you can count on our prayers for Sonny as well."

Before Cody could make a reply, his cell phone rang. "Oh my! I was hoping not to be disturbed, but we're having plumbing problems and on Saturday of all days. This is probably Anna wanting me to talk with the plumber. Hello...yes—what?" Then gasping, he said, "How bad?"

Weeda and Kyle, shocked by the anxiety in Cody's voice, started quietly praying for whatever the problem might be. Cody, having turned pale and looking stunned, pushed the off button and blurted out. "It's about Sally. She was in that accident that held you up. She's in surgery at Providence. Anna is already there, so I'll have to leave. The woman has no immediate family, just a niece and a nephew in Birmingham." He pulled himself together and while going through the door, turned and whispered, "Do pray."

"Of course, and we'll be in touch. You have Weeda's phone number. We'll probably follow you as soon as we can lock up and make a couple of calls."

Sally had been in surgery about an hour when Weeda and Kyle joined Cody and Anna in the waiting room. Cody was staring into space and Anna was quietly praying. Kyle took a seat next to Cody and spoke to him softly, almost inaudibly to which Cody responded in a voice for all to hear.

"It's bad, very bad. The informer—I forget what she called herself—just left. She said the doctors are doing all they can, but her condition is listed as critical. A SUV ran a red light and broadsided her squarely on the driver's side. Nobody else in the car. The SUV driver was hurt, but is going to be all right. So bad! So bad! Why? Why?"

"Questions come easy at times like this," replied Kyle, "but answers don't." He regretted he couldn't be of more comfort, but how could he comfort when he himself was so uncomfortable? "Mr. Houston, I'm at a loss for answers, but we are here to help. Anybody we can contact for you? Her relatives in Birmingham?"

"Thanks, but Sally's assistant is making those calls. My main concern is Sonny. They have not been able to locate him. Even in his present confused state, I know he'd be here if he knew."

"What about Ms. Sheldon's minister? Has he been notified?"

Speaking softly and slowly, Anna shook her head. "That's part of my heartache. Sally never joined a church—never felt a need to profess any particular belief, but she was so fine, such a helpful and caring person. Once in a while she did attend some special functions with a friend at that little Episcopal church on Dellisville Road—St. Andrews, I believe. I feel so guilty that since we've been so taken up with concerns for Sonny that I've been remiss in praying for her. Maybe if I had..." She didn't finish her thought.

Weeda and Kyle exchanged glances indicating they would like to ease Anna's concern by telling her about Sally's conversion, but that was Cody's prerogative, and he remained silent, so they did likewise.

A young lady came through the door and approached Cody. "Mr. Houston, we've learned that Sonny has gone with a group from Woodland High School to some kind of rally in Saxton, so we're unable to track him down, but we'll keep trying."

"Thank you, Gracey." Then, turning to Weeda and Kyle, he said, "Ms. McVey, Dr. Sanders, this is Gracey Lee, Ms. Sheldon's assistant. Gracey, these are professional friends of mine."

"Yes," said Gracey. "I've met you, Dr. Sanders. You probably don't recall because I've always remained in the waiting room while my mother sees you. You're her internist."

They were on the verge of recalling specific connections when the door opened and in walked the doctor. Everyone read his face and knew what he was about to say but didn't know just how he would say it. Nodding in their direction, he said, "Mr. Houston, Mrs. Houston, I'm Dr. Wells, the surgeon on call. I'm sorry to have to tell you that Ms. Sheldon died a few minutes ago. We did our best, but it wasn't good enough. She suffered severe internal injuries and the bleeding was profuse. Had we been able to extend her life, I doubt she could have completely recovered. Again, I'm so sorry. The hospital will have a staff member here shortly to assist you—to take your instructions." He recognized Kyle who at times had assisted him in the operating room. They chatted briefly, and he left.

* * *

Weeda's alarm went off at seven. She quickly shut it off, fighting the urge to turn over and sleep in on this Sunday morning. Certainly she could use some rest after all the stress of yesterday and last night. She wrestled with the sleep-in temptation a little longer then suddenly remembered something—the obituaries. Pulling herself out of bed and slipping into her robe, she stepped outside, picked up the *Rushton Register* and flipped to the obits. There it was:

Sally Marie Sheldon, 48; resident of Rushton for 25 years; daughter of the late Jackson and Avie Sheldon; executive secretary of Houston Enterprises; survived by a nephew, Curvin H. Sheldon, and a niece, Christy Sheldon Giles, both of Birmingham; preceded in death by her parents and a brother, Herman T. Sheldon; local private funeral to be followed by burial service in Birmingham.

On Sunday, Weeda usually read through the paper before dressing for church, but this morning she laid it aside and sat sipping hot tea and munching on cinnamon toast. Last night's events kept rumbling through her mind.

She and Kyle had left the hospital waiting room as more of Cody's employees came in. Later they met Cody and Anna at Sally's place but departed when Sally's relatives arrived. There still had been no word of Sonny when they departed, which was puzzling because the Woodland High group was already back in town. Other than the Houstons, only she and Kyle seemed anxious about Sonny's whereabouts, but why should his employees be concerned? After all, in their thinking, Sally was just one among many on Cody's payroll. She had to remind herself that the others had no inkling that the deceased was Sonny's mother.

She needed to get moving to get ready for church, but she felt so lethargic and heavy hearted, wondering if Sonny really knew the rock-bottom truth—that he was Sally's son. When he had first confided in her about the adoption discovery, he was guarded and vague about how much he had found out. She had assumed he knew the specifics, but he certainly had not identified his biological parents by name. Come to think of it, he had not made known to her just what he had seen. If what he had seen was the certificate of adoption, then he had to know. How then, she wondered, was he going to react to Sally's death?

Also, she wondered if by now Cody had told Anna about Sally's salvation experience. Probably not, since revealing it might open up questions he was not ready to answer. She felt for Cody.

Surely his emotional and mental stamina was being tested. She prayed that his newfound faith would sustain him and that God would use this crisis to bring good into Sonny and Anna's lives. She needed to talk to Kyle but hesitated to disturb him. Anyway, her time was short. She would probably hear from him this afternoon. On Sunday evenings they usually attended church service together except when he was on call, and that was not the case this weekend.

* * *

As she had expected, Kyle called in the afternoon and suggested they skip church and spend the evening together at his place.

She arrived at dusk and they sat in front of the fire munching on pizza bites, pepper poppers, and some of Evanne's home-baked cookies. Weeda commented on the cookies and asked about Evanne.

"She never ceases to amaze me," he replied. "She's the same and yet not the same and doesn't fit into any mold I've ever observed or studied. In conversation, she seems completely devoid of humor and is always as literal as a signpost, but the woman offsets that image when she writes her thoughts on paper. I'm never here when she takes her breaks, but I find bits and pieces of writings that she claims she jots down when she drinks her mid-morning coffee and her afternoon soda. She leaves scribbles around, apparently to get my comments."

"You've mentioned that before. What are the scribbles like?"

"I'll let you be the judge," and reaching into the drawer of the coffee table, he pulled out a sheet of paper from a lined yellow pad. "Listen to this. She can't spell, and her writing is worse than my prescriptions, but I've read this over several times, so I don't have to guess at it. Here goes:

> *Nellie Sue fell in love and planned to marrie Joe.*
> *She bes so happy bout it and tell her pappy so,*
> *But Pappy say, Hole on, slo doun, you hafta fine another,*
> *Don't let yur mama no but Joe is yo halve brother.*
> *So Nellie set aside her Joe and plan to marrie Will,*
> *But Pappy say, hole on, slo doun, there's yet a problem still.*
> *Again I say, keep it secret from yo mother*
> *But Will like Joe is alsew yur halve brother.*
> *Now Mama did fine out and this is what she said*
> *My child, do whatever will make you happy*
> *Marrie Will or marrie Joe cause you ant no ken to Pappy.*

Weeda laughed so hard she could scarcely find words, "Kyle are you sure Evanne wrote that—that she didn't get that verse somewhere else and copy it as her own?"

"I've asked her as much, but she says she just likes to write down what pops into her head, that she has always done it."

"Do you have any other pieces?"

"No, but after I came across this one I decided to save any others I find. Who knows? The woman may one day be noted for her red-necked verses."

"I thought red-necks were white."

"I suppose you're right, but this sounds red-necked to me. Well, enough of that. What's on your mind?"

"You know."

"When's the funeral?"

"I don't know. According to the paper, it's to be private, so I don't suppose the time will be announced. I haven't heard from anyone. I'm just wondering about Sonny, whether or not he is on the scene yet and if so, how he is reacting."

"Yes, I know that does concern you."

"Do you think I should inquire?"

"That's up to you. As for myself, I don't think so. In the event Cody comes to us for more counseling, we need to be as objective in our advice as possible by reacting not so much to what we know about his situation from personal observation and involvement but from what he tells us. It's his perspective the Lord is seeking to make right, and we have to deal with him from his perspective to determine how closely his thinking squares or fails to square with God's guidelines. Right or wrong?"

"You're right, and besides, I didn't know Sally, and until all this came up, I didn't know Cody and Anna except through the church."

"I suspect Cody had much to do with keeping the funeral private."

"Sure, and for good reasons."

"Whew! Just think of it. All these complications in Cody's life as a result of having made some wrong decisions, but of course, much wrong thinking preceded those decisions. Makes me want to pray earnestly and often, 'Lord, lead me not to my own counsel, but to yours.'"

"Have you always asked for that kind of guidance?"

"Are you kidding? Not until long after I became a Christian."

"Recently, you promised to tell me more about your pre-Christian life. This might be a good time to keep that promise. We've talked at length about my past, but not yours."

"I doubt my memory will serve me well. I have fairly good recall when it comes to the positives but when it comes to the negatives, not so good."

"That's supposed to be a sure sign of good mental health, isn't it?"

"Hopefully so, unless one takes the tendency too far and goes into denial. Anyway, my recall might not be too conducive to objectivity, and I'm sure you want the truth."

"Kyle, you're taking me on a rabbit chase. Let's get down to specifics. Did you always want to be a doctor?"

"I'm not sure when I started thinking about medicine. My dad wanted me to go into the business, but I was never interested in being a businessman. I wanted to be a professional person—to use my mind. Success in business requires certain drives I don't have."

"Such as?"

"For one thing, the urge to accumulate. I naturally want whatever it takes to live comfortably with some assurance of security, but possessions can be such a burden. I've seen my dad labor under that load all my life. And look at Cody. Look at what he did for the sake of keeping the family possessions intact."

"You have a timely argument there."

"I don't disdain ownership nor do I make any claims to the virtues of poverty, and I certainly don't regard money as filthy lucre. I'm not talking about people who go into business to make a living. I'm talking about those who have more than they need but are afflicted with an inordinate desire to accumulate more, business people who allow themselves to be victimized by greed and pride. That's what happened to Cody."

"You mentioned your dad. The few times I've been around him, I didn't detect those qualities in him."

"Fortunately, he has handled his business with fewer complications than has Cody, but even so, his work as taken its toll on his spiritual life. Even at this advancing age, he remains a nominal Christian because through the years he has traded off spiritual endeavors and has sacrificed the better things at the altar of success. Along those lines, I often think of the well-known coach who was a committed Christian and worked hard at keeping his priorities on a spiritual basis. He said he was not afraid of failure. What he feared was attaining success in things that really didn't matter in the long haul of life."

"Sobering thoughts."

"Anyway, back to Dad. Lately I'm seeing some changes as he takes on more and more of my mom's priorities. God is answering our prayers."

"I know you're grateful for the changes. Now about those negatives you don't recall so well."

He thought for a while, then answered. "I was selfish and probably still am—not about things but with my time. As is often the case, Providence has worked in my behalf. As a doctor, the temptation to use my time selfishly is greatly reduced because there is so little of it."

"But Kyle, you make time for Bible study, so I don't see how you can say you're selfish with you time."

"But I can't count that as a plus from a personal standpoint since that time belongs to the Lord initially. It would be robbery to utilize it apart from His purposes. I think Christians are obligated to give of their time just as they give of their substance. Personally, about the only way I ever utilized my free time was fishing, and since I met you, I've subtracted from the fishing time and given it to you."

"I hope you're not regretting it."

"Of course not. You're giving your time to me. It's a sharing and one I enjoy."

She was determined to keep him talking about his past and questioned him again. "Were there ever other women with whom you enjoyed sharing your time?"

"Are you asking if I've ever been in love?"

"You just won't let me indulge in subtleties, will you? OK, I'll put it bluntly. Have you ever been in love?"

"Yes, once. When I was in medical school."

"Can you tell me about it?"

"There's not a great deal to tell. She had a beautiful alliterative name—Nelda Nevins. She was a journalist, a newspaper reporter. Her assignments included covering the medical school. That's how we met. We dated for about a year and became engaged when I finished school."

"What happened?"

"It's still hard to talk about, but you have a right to know. The summer I finished my internship she was drowned off the coast of Maine while visiting relatives who had a summer cottage there."

She was flabbergasted. "Kyle, I'm so sorry. I feel so bad. We've spent so much time on my emotional hurts and none on yours. You must have been devastated."

After a lengthy silence, he let out a long sigh. "It was rough, and in trying to overcome, I probably utilized defense mechanisms not even mentioned in the psych books. Fighting anger and bitterness was my constant companion—a phantom tiger. That's probably the reason I felt for you when I saw you building a wall around yourself, cutting yourself off from another relationship. I had been there, but fortunately I knew the Lord and eventually I garnered enough humility to ask for his help and went for prayer counseling, but not before I had tried to macho the experience, pretending I could handle whatever life threw my way. That effort proved to be an exercise in futility. With God's help and a medical residency program that allowed no time for self-absorption and introspection, I weathered the ordeal."

"Do you think you're completely healed?"

"If you delete the adverb, I like to think so. Otherwise, I can't speak with that much certainly. I remember thinking soon after Nelda's death that love brings a grafting, the melding of two people together, and in my case, when she died I felt as though a part of me had been amputated, that I was actually minus something in a physical sense. You remember that minus feeling, I'm sure?"

"Yes, but after that session with the Corleys, it became a 'thank goodness' kind of minus. I don't think yours would fall into that category." They fell silent, both lost in reveries. After an extended mulling, Weeda broke the silence. "Maybe this isn't the appropriate time to bring it up, but a few weeks ago at Westwinds, you—"

He cut her off. "Yeah, I know. I spelled out certain stipulations about any such relationship in the future. Do you remember those stipulations?"

"How could I forget?"

"How do feel about them now?"

"As you know, I was angry at first, but after you explained yourself—that you were concerned for my spiritual well being—I must say that such depth of concern expressed in my behalf overwhelmed me. I was so moved to think that a man whom I admired could regard me so unselfishly."

With their backs against the coffee table, they sat side by side on the floor watching the burning embers. Kyle reached over and pulled her to himself, her shoulders and upper body cradled in his arms, and looking down into her eyes, he whispered.

"So many times I've wanted to really kiss you, yearning with more feeling than I could allow myself to show. My affections have been guarded, sufficing with just little goodnight kisses." After those words, he kissed her with such tender passion that she knew every negative feeling and attitude she had ever retained were being cancelled in this one protracted mingling, not just flesh with flesh but spirit with spirit. For the first time in her life, she was experiencing a completeness she had never thought possible. She knew this was more than physical love, that the very God of Heaven was showing His love for her through this man. How could her racing thoughts ever be verbally expressed?

Kyle's lips left hers as he pulled her against his chest again. Words were inadequate, so they didn't even try to talk. Finally stirring, she whispered, "Kyle I can't explain what's going on but—"

"Neither can I, but I suspect that by coming together, two broken hearts are being healed. Love cures all kinds of maladies and mends fractured lives." Then, after tenderly kissing her again, he whispered, "Dear, I'd love to spend this night with you, but that would he putting my emotional desires above your spiritual welfare. Besides, it is my responsibility to protect your reputation. So I'm sending you home. I'll see you to the car, and you call as soon as you get there."

When she reached her place, she phoned, saying, "Kyle, my heart is so full of gratitude. How can I ever thank you?"

"Don't try, just give your heart to God, and I'll petition Him to share a portion of it with me. That's all I ask. Night, Dear."

"Goodnight, Kyle."

* * *

The events of last evening had put Weeda on Cloud Nine, and on this Monday morning it seemed as though she was still floating around up there somewhere. Try as she would, she just couldn't come down to the mundane. Although she was getting things done, her performance was perfunctory as though her automatic cruise button had been pushed, but that button was somehow released when Ms. Larson announced that Macy Bryant was waiting to see her. In her euphoric daze, she had failed to notice that Macy's name had been inserted on today's schedule. Before she could lament further, Macy was in the office explaining her reason for coming.

"Ms. McVey, we have everything squared away to begin the Bible study. Dad has made arrangements for us to use the chapel at Morningside Methodist every second and fourth Saturday from ten til twelve. The minister gave us the chapel because it's a smaller area to heat or cool on off-work days."

Though the news was good, Weeda was not ready to take on one more assignment, not even in a supportive way, but she dare not put a damper on the enthusiasm she saw on the girl's face and picked up in her voice, so she made an effort to have her words belie her feelings. "Good, wonderful! My! You're a pro at getting things organized. I'll make a note of that in your cumulative file."

"Gee, thanks. But Mom and Dad have done most of the work. Fifty-two have registered, and of the study topics Dr. Sanders offered to teach, thirty chose 'Bible Answers to Puzzling Questions.' I'm pleased about that. That was my choice."

Weeda picked up her scribble pad. "Let me make some notes to pass on to Dr. Sanders."

"You don't need to. I called Mom , and she has already given all the info to him by phone this morning. He told her he could start a week from Saturday. He also said that a man from Dellisville will sub if he is needed."

"Yes, that's Mr. Corley. He's quite a Bible scholar."

Though her verbalizing effort was still more or less on cruise, suddenly she found herself trying to formulate an inquiry concerning Sonny. She still had not heard anything and wondered if Macy was aware of the circumstances and might know of any recent developments. She resisted the urge to ask, thinking it unwise to open up a discussion that might lead down a path she dare not go, so they quickly went over the Bible study plans again, readily agreeing that the Bryants would continue to serve as sponsors.

"Everybody involved in this effort is indebted to your parents, Macy. I'll call your mother this evening and express my gratitude."

While Weeda continued to talk, Macy was walking toward the door to leave. Suddenly she stopped, turned around and said, "Ms. McVey, isn't it strange about Sonny? Mr. Houston called me last night hoping I might know something, but I couldn't help him. He said Sonny left town with a group from Woodland on Saturday but didn't return with them, and he hasn't heard anything from him since. He was really upset. Said he had a private investigator looking into the situation. I don't think he's in school today."

"Yes, I know the Houstons were concerned about him Saturday night, and I haven't heard anything since. I'm glad to know about the investigator—hope they can help get to the bottom of Sonny's changed behavior. Mr. Houston's secretary was killed in a traffic accident on Saturday, adding to their stress and anxiety. I feel for them."

"Yes, Mr. Houston mentioned her death when he called and said he and others from his company would be in Birmingham for the burial service on Tuesday—tomorrow. He also said he was keeping the investigation on the QT, so I haven't mentioned it to anyone but you. I can't believe I'm so calm about Sonny. A few weeks ago this would have turned me inside out. I must be getting over him."

"Sounds like it, and no doubt that pleases your parents."

"That's for sure. I think they've been busy, praying him out of my life. They believe in the power of prayer."

"What a blessing to have such parents. I wish more of our young people could benefit from a heritage such as yours. I really am concerned about Sonny though, so if you hear anything else, will you call me?"

"Sure thing," she said as she exited the door.

* * *

After her bath, Weeda settled down with one of Eudora Welty's novels. If anybody could rivet her attention, Welty could, and she definitely needed something to distract her from the fixations that had controlled her thinking for three days. Since Sunday evening she had spent every free moment reliving the events of that night with Kyle or wondering about Sonny. This was Tuesday—three days had passed and he was still gone.

Sometimes it puzzled her that she could or would allow herself to become overly absorbed with certain counselees. For some time it had been Sonny, Hammie, and Macy. They were stuck to her or her to them like a postage stamp on a postal card. After things had become resolved for Sonny, if they ever did, she wondered who would take his place. Recently he and his problems had been much too absorbing. He had been on the absentee list again today, but so far as she knew nobody had questioned his absence, probably because colds and flu were making their rounds so three or four missed days were not unusual. But the fact that he was missing from home was another matter. She so wanted to find out something, but Kyle felt it unwise to inquire. For several reasons, she considered his advice worth the taking. He was knowledgeable and he was wise, and that wisdom enabled him to utilize his knowledge well. Also, he had the ability to extract any and all selfishness from his counsel; consequently, the advice he rendered was free of ulterior motives. The upshot was: he could be trusted.

"Wow! Here I go again," she uttered aloud, "getting intoxicated with thoughts of this man." She needed help, so she started praying.

"Lord, You'll have to help me keep my balance where this man is concerned. Slow me down. Help me to be practical. Help me to control my emotions. Although Kyle makes suggestions about a lasting relationship, he hasn't actually proposed, and knowing him, it may take him months, even years—heaven forbid—to get to the place I am. In fact, he might just go back to those little non-emotional 'peck-on-the-cheek' kind of kisses. Don't let him do that. If you don't help me, I might just lose control and make a fool of myself. I thought I was going to read Welty, but here I am, crying out to You, asking You to keep me in line emotionally and mentally. After that devastating marital experience with Lanny, I wondered if I could ever be aroused again. That Sunday night experience with Kyle has put that concern to rest, and I find myself going in the opposite direction. The way I'm now reacting to Kyle, I might have to ask You to put on my brakes—the brakes to my libido, that is..."

The telephone rang. It was Macy.

"Ms. McVey, you asked me to call if I learned any thing about Sonny."

"Yes," she gasped, "by all means, tell me."

"He called about an hour ago. He was home but very upset that his folks were not there. Said he called his dad's secretary to find out their whereabouts but didn't get an answer. I didn't know what to say, so I told him they were probably still in Birmingham. I'm afraid I did wrong by telling him why they were there."

"Don't be so hard on yourself. What was his reaction?"

"Oh! I thought he was going bonkers. That's why I feel so bad about it. I think I was out of line. Somebody else should have delivered that message. It was really strange, as though a member of his family had died."

Weeda had to brake her tongue to keep from saying too much, so she shifted to: "What else did he say? Did he tell you where he had been?"

"I asked that question, but he said he couldn't say—said there were a lot of things he couldn't explain, and he said something else that was really puzzling. Said he wouldn't be back in school, that he wouldn't be leaving the house. I was afraid to ask any more questions, so I just told him I was glad he was back home and that my parents and I had been praying for him. He kinda choked up, saying we shouldn't waste our breath on such. I still believe he's on drugs, and I'm beginning to wonder if it might be even worse than that."

"Like what?"

"I don't know. Do you think he has done something criminal?"

"Heaven forbid, but the situation does sound grim."

"My dad has gone to talk to our pastor—wants to get his advice. He's leery of getting involved with things that concern Mr. Houston, but he wants to do something for Sonny, and he feels he can trust Pastor Pritchard's judgment."

Weeda was in a quandary about what to say. "Do you know whether or not Sonny tried his dad's cell phone number?"

"No, that wasn't mentioned."

"Macy, I do feel we should pray for Sonny before we hang up."

"Sure."

Weeda prayed. "Dear Lord, we're deeply troubled for Sonny. We don't know the details of his plight, but you do. So the two of us are standing in the gap, trusting that our standing will make a difference. Will you send angelic assistance to either keep or remove him from harm's way—perhaps from doing violence to himself if that's in his mind? Bring his parents home safely and give them wisdom about dealing with his plight. I'm making these requests in the mighty and powerful name of Jesus. Amen."

They hung up. Immediately, she rang Kyle's number, but there was no answer. Very likely, he was making his hospital rounds. Though unsettling to say the least, Macy's call had certainly quenched her smoldering libido.

She picked up the novel, wondering if even Welty could take her mind away from what she had just learned from Macy.

* * *

Wednesday was a routine day, that is, until Ms. Larson announced that Cody Houston had called during lunch period and was on his way over.

"On his way here? But he doesn't have an appointment, and I have a full schedule this afternoon."

"I tried to tell him as much, but he didn't listen. Said you'd understand. So I just grunted a 'un huh' which means he's on his way." Weeda's pursing lips, raised eyebrows, and a slight nodding of the head told her something was going on and she was not in on the know, so she asked, "Shall I cancel the appointment for the next hour?"

"Not only for the next hour but for the afternoon."

It was her time to raise the eyebrows, which she did, but managed to stifle the questions she wanted to ask: What's going on? Why do you get flustered every time C. H. comes on the scene, and why does Sonny never come in any more, even when he is summoned with an invitational pass? She paced back to her desk, perturbed that Mr. C. H. was throwing his weight around here at school the same as elsewhere. "Oh well," she said to herself, "I'd better just keep quiet, but that won't keep me from using my hawk eyes."

Cody arrived and immediately got down to business as soon as the office door was closed. "I apologize for barging in like this, but I need to see you and Dr. Sanders right away for a prayer session. I need to take some action immediately, but I don't know what action to take."

"I'm sure you're right on that score. I hear Sonny is back home. What's going on with him?"

"That's what we don't know. He has us frightened. When we came back last night from the burial, he was home but doesn't tell us a thing except to say he won't be going back to school."

"He doesn't give reasons?"

"None. In fact, he won't talk at all. He's a basket case. Came out of his room only to grab a sandwich. Anna is beside herself, and all this at a time when I wanted to square with her about my deceptive past."

"Sounds as though things are coming to a head and fast. You need to get some truthful dialogue going with that son of yours."

"I couldn't agree more. I suggested to him in the kindest way I could that we needed to talk, but in a desultory manner he let me know he wouldn't ask me any questions if I wouldn't ask him any, then he was right back in his room with the door locked. He knows something, and I'm wondering how much he knows."

"It's time you found out."

"Do you suppose—is there any way you and Dr. Sanders could see me this afternoon or this evening? I have to take some action. I think the boy needs to be hospitalized. I thought of calling the family doctor, but he doesn't know the situation, about what's going on, and Sanders does. I tried calling Sanders but he wasn't in his office, and they wouldn't give me his private number. I'm sure you have it."

"Yes. But I don't give it out either. But let's see. Today is Wednesday, and he's off for the afternoon. I'll call and see if he's home." She rang both his home and cell numbers but received no answer and explained that he was probably fishing. She promised that she'd keep trying to reach him.

"Please do, and I'll meet you wherever you say."

"One more thing," she replied. "You need to bring Anna. Dealing with these problems in a piece-meal fashion is no longer an option. You and Anna need to be of one mind when you confront Sonny concerning his rebellion, especially his school attendance."

"You're right. You're right. That means—well…"

"It means the unknowns between you and Anna must be made known prior to your confrontation with Sonny."

"I can receive that, but do I square things away with her before we get with you or during the session?"

"Why don't you ask the Lord to orchestrate for you?"

"Yes, yes, of course. You have my phone numbers. I'll wait to hear from you."

* * *

At seven o'clock that evening the four of them met in Kyle's outer office. Kyle, still in his fishing garb, set the stage, briefly outlining the procedure to be followed. He gave Cody and Anna each some notepaper on which to define the problems they were facing, asking them to identify, if possible, the underlying cause or causes of their difficulties and to state how and to what degree they intended to seek God in searching for solutions. He also asked them to make their statements independently, without any communication between themselves.

Immediately after he had finished his directions, he and Weeda withdrew to the inner office where she filled him in on the latest developments. Their cell phone conversation late that afternoon had of necessity been brief, just long enough to set up a time and place and to agree that Anna's attendance was a must. Kyle knew nothing about the latest details.

She started by saying, "Cody barged in to see me at school today without an appointment. He was so distraught. Sonny is back home but in a state of silent rebellion, refusing to go to school but not giving a reason. He stays in his room, not coming out except to grab a sandwich and to warn Cody against any prying. In fact, to quote him directly, he said, 'I won't ask you any questions if you won't ask me any.'"

"Defining his parameters, huh?"

She nodded and continued. "Also, things between Cody and Anna are still the same: Cody hasn't confessed anything. So Anna still doesn't know about Sally's accepting the Lord. How the two of them have lived together all these years with such a plethora of unknowns between them is beyond me."

"Yeah! But when one lives a lie long enough, the lie becomes reality to the liar and his performance is adjusted accordingly. In your professional parlance, you'd probably refer to it as 'performance orientation.' Anyway, if Cody deals with these questions squarely and honestly, then we might better prepare ourselves for some high drama because I expect them to share their responses openly."

"Good! I told Cody this afternoon that he had to come clean with Anna—that it's imperative that they be of one mind when they confront Sonny, especially concerning school attendance."

At that point they ceased talking and started praying, asking the Lord to orchestrate the session, that truth would surface, causing Cody to be honest and to then furnish Anna with the grace to receive that honesty, that forgiveness would follow the confession, flowing downward from the Lord and back and forth between Anna and Cody.

After they had prayed, they sat quietly, looking at one another, each wondering what the other was thinking. "A penny for your thoughts, Kyle."

"I can't believe it. I was about to ask you the same thing."

"Then I'll go first. I was wondering if you resent my bringing you into all these counseling situations. They're as time consuming as a major medical operation and leave you no time for Bible study."

"I do admit I'm frustrated when I'm unable to study the Word, but no, I don't resent having been brought into this situation because I feel it is of the Lord, not only for the benefit of the counselees but for ours as well. Learning from the written Word is great, but seeing that Word produce fruit in the lives of others is even greater. These are good learning experiences."

"I couldn't agree more. This kind of work just shows that the Word of God is alive and powerful—Hebrews 4:12 in evidence."

"Yeah! And such a faith builder, not just for the counselee but for those who minister."

"So true. My appreciation for the Scriptures has increased so much since I learned about this ministry."

"Yes, I know. You're growing by leaps and bounds."

"I hope so, and I'm glad you've noticed. Eventually, I may be able to measure up to those standards you specify."

"Oh, come on. You make me sound like a stuffed shirt with a legalistic work-ethic mentality."

"I didn't mean it that way, though come to think of it, you might be just a smidgen guilty as to the latter."

"Are you saying I come across as one who thinks salvation is gained through works? I hope not. I'll have to rethink about how my words are perceived. I certainly don't want to come across that way." He glanced toward the outer room. "I think they've finished. What's coming up could turn out to be a testing, not only of our faith but also of our ability to use the Scriptures to liberate those in bondage. Would you like to take the lead?"

"You can't be serious. I'm seeking Christian maturity; that's for sure, but I'm not hankering to take the final test anytime soon."

They found Anna sitting quietly with her eyes closed, her papers on the table, as though in prayer. Cody was looking down, pretending to be rereading what he had penned. He cleared his throat several times, an action Kyle interpreted as a stalling tactic and said, "If you need more time, go ahead and take it. We can check back later."

"No, I've finished what little I had to say. If your purpose was to shake me up, you've succeeded. I've written very little, but I've been forced to think, and the thinking has me under conviction again."

"Good! Conviction is a work of the Holy Spirit, and when He gets activated, things begin to happen. We're believing for that, aren't we, Weeda?"

She agreed, and Kyle quickly turned his attention to Anna. "And you, Mrs. Houston, you go first. What is your main reason for coming here today?"

"I've tried to think through these questions, and I'll have to say that I'm here for several reasons, but my immediate concern is Sonny. We have some serious personal problems, but those have to take a back seat to Sonny's predicament. The boy needs to recover his sanity. I'm wondering if he doesn't need hospitalization, and if so, can you aid us in getting that help?"

"I can appreciate what you're asking, and we'll certainly give Sonny's predicament priority, but I'm wondering: Do you suppose the personal problems you just alluded to might be a contributing factor to Sonny's rebellion? Children are never isolated from the concerns of the parents. They are caught up in them whether we are aware of it or not."

"I'm sure you're right, but I won't go into all the ins and outs since Cody says he has discussed Sonny's behavioral changes with both of you in previous sessions. The truth is he's just getting worse. He's a basket case. We need to take some action now." Cody, slightly biting his upper lip, nodded in agreement.

"I understand what you're saying, Mrs. Houston, but let's get back. What do you think is the underlying cause of Sonny's rebellion?"

She sat very still, eyes closed as though she wanted to shut out the harsh reality of what needed to be said. "I don't know, unless maybe he resents…I'm hesitant to say."

"Go ahead. Success in these sessions hinges on your being candid."

"That we have not been forthright with him about some things."

"Such as?"

Cody perked up, his head tilted in Anna's direction, a surprised look on his face, as though he was afraid of what might be said next. She continued. "Can parents afford to be completely honest with their children, human nature being what it is? We're not selfless; we're selfish." She hesitated, but Kyle, sensing she was being evasive, pressed on.

"Go ahead. What blame, if any, are you willing to assume?"

"Well, there's the adoption issue." Cody stiffened but remained quiet except for the continuous clearing of the throat.

"What about the adoption issue?"

"We were never honest with Sonny." She spoke calmly but deliberately. "I believe the time has come that we must level with him and tell him the truth about the adoption."

Cody flushed a rosy hue but remained quiet except for the continuous shifting of the eyes from Anna to Kyle to Weeda and back to Kyle.

"That's interesting," said Kyle. "Since he has long known that he is adopted, are you telling me he's wanting to find his birth parents?"

"Not that. I think he has become suspicious about the adoption, and if so, it's possible he has figured out who his birth parents are."

Cody's blush instantly vanished and a blanching set in. He was white even behind the ears, all color going with the blood down to his racing heart and churning stomach. He attempted to speak, but Kyle signaled him to silence. "Please continue, Mrs. Houston."

Nodding toward her husband, she said, "I've been waiting, hoping Cody would see the need to reveal some truths to the boy and to me, but I've waited long enough. As I said, I believe Sonny has found out about his parentage. I can't tell you why I feel that way. I just do."

Weeda was fluttering inside and wanted to shout "Amen" but managed to maintain her composure as well as her silence, knowing Kyle would hold out for the rock-bottom details.

Cody didn't do that well with his emotions. He ignored Kyle's signals for silence and blurted out, "Anna, what are you saying? What things?"

The atmosphere was thick with stirred-up feelings that couldn't be harnessed and Kyle's format for the session was submerged in a sea of fervor, not to be retrieved. The counselors became mere onlookers to a drama which had taken on a momentum all it own. They were witnessing a confession the likes of which they had never observed in their professional experiences. To Anna and Cody it was as though they were alone, free of any observations. Cody continued with his rattling questions. "But how? Where? When did you find out whatever it is you claim you found out?"

"When Sonny was about a year old."

"But you never let on."

"No, for the good of everybody, I decided to live with it. I thought it best for you, for Sally, for myself, and for Sonny. And everything went smoothly until a few months ago."

"But Anna, what, tell me, did you find out?"

"You know full well what I found out. I found out that you and Sally begat a child whom you pretended to adopt. That's what I found out."

"But how? Where? Who?"

"Sorry, Mr. Houston, it's now my time to be secretive. You've had your turn, so I'm not saying how I learned about your clandestine shenanigans."

"But did you not care that I had—"

"Been unfaithful? Sure. I was crushed, but can you imagine what the results might have been had I exposed you? So I sought the Lord continuously for several weeks. Then forgiveness set in, not only toward you but also toward Sally, and she became one of my best friends. I came to love her as a sister. I so wanted her to know the Lord."

"Anna, your prayers were answered. Sally accepted the Lord about a week before she was killed, right in my office."

"Cody," her voice cracked, "why didn't you tell me? This is almost more than I can take in. How did it happen?"

Cody was slow to answer, trying to winnow his words. "Anna, I've been trying to come clean about my past ever since Sonny started on this downward spiral, knowing that for his sake I had to do what to me seemed impossible—confess and shape up. These two sitting here can vouch for that. I had told them about the deceptions, and in the process of my sordid confession, I myself was saved. Sally noticed the changes that salvation had wrought so she wanted the same for herself. She sought the Lord, and in His faithfulness, He gloriously saved her. In fact, before she died, she was on fire for the things of God, seeking Him with all her heart."

Anna was silent for some time; then speaking in a soft whisper as if to herself, "How I thank him for answered prayer. That explains her call to me on Thursday before the accident on Saturday. She said she had something good to share and wanted me to meet her for lunch on Monday, but that Monday didn't come for her. So sad, but how blessed I am that God has answered my petitions for both you and her." Wiping away tears, she continued: "It's impossible to say what I feel. Adultery and deceptions, though sinful, lose their wounding power when placed under the blood and forgiving love of Jesus Christ."

Cody sat looking at his wife as though she were an apparition, a verbalizing spirit not to be touched, but with such an expression of gratitude and forgiveness, he couldn't refrain. He pulled his chair over and put his arm around her. She responded by stroking his quivering chin. In deference, Kyle and Weeda dropped their gaze, feeling awkward as though their presence was an intrusion, but they had no intention of withdrawing. Too much prayer, time, and concern had been invested to walk away and miss out on what seemed to be the beginning of a solution to an otherwise insurmountable problem. Though they were not looking, they heard Cody say, "Anna, I came here today fully intending to confess all my deceiving schemes of the past and to ask your forgiveness. I had no idea you knew—that you had forgiven me long ago. I don't know how—I don't know how to say what needs to be said."

"Then don't try. We have no choice but to forget about ourselves. We must concentrate on Sonny. It's an emergency, Cody. It's an emergency."

"I know. I know. But if you can forgive me, then I'm going to trust that Sonny can too. But, Anna, I'm afraid Sonny's difficulty extends far beyond the secrets and sins connected to his birth."

"You're right, but I don't have a clue as to what they are. Something very sinister is going on with that boy."

Sighing and barely able to speak, Cody turned to Kyle, "Dr. Sanders, we—I need direction. How can I come clean with Sonny when he won't even talk to me, or listen? He walks away when I try to approach him. I'm ready to confess but unless there's a change, there's no way."

Weeda spoke up. "Why don't you try writing him a letter? Just pour your heart out on paper." Kyle nodded in silence, remembering quite well how Weeda had used the postal service to bridge the chasm when their relationship had reached an impasse. Cody ceased eye contact and stared long and hard toward the corner of the room. After a time he pursed his lips and slightly nodded his head, giving some indication of consent. "You just might be onto to something. It's worth a try. I'm ready to do whatever it takes. I'll sequester myself tonight until I have on paper what's pent up in my heart and needs to come out. Will you please be in prayer for me? We do so covet your prayers and your willingness to help us come through."

"Sure thing," said Kyle. "Give the letter a try and keep us informed. We'll walk with you to the parking lot."

* * *

Approximately fifty students assembled for the first Bible study on Saturday morning. Macy's father, Mr. Bryant, made the introductions and explained the procedures to be followed, and then Kyle took his place before the group.

From among several topical choices, the students had chosen "Bible Answers to Puzzling Questions" as the theme for the study. Today's question read: "How do we as Christians defend our belief in creation when archaeological findings indicate that the age of the earth and prehistoric man predate the creation account as recorded in Genesis?"

Before he addressed the question, Kyle congratulated the students for putting forth the effort to study the Bible. At that moment he saw Weeda slip quietly through the side door and take a seat apart from the group. She was flushed, still in her jogging suit. He was glad she had arrived in time to critique his teaching. He felt confident in dealing with the subject matter but not so sure about presenting the material to that age group. He briefly called attention to Weeda's presence. They all clapped, and he continued with his commendations.

"Again, I want to commend you for giving of your time to learn from the greatest of all books. Time wise, it's the best endeavor you will ever pursue. Let me briefly tell you why this is true.

"The Bible can make claims no other book can make. Why? Because it was written under the inspiration of the Third Person of the Godhead, who possesses, along with God the Father and God the Son, the means by which man can come to know God. It is superior to all other books for satisfying the soul since it provides the only fail-safe compass for extending life beyond the grave. It is an authorized handbook on the affairs of daily life, simple in its presentation but profound in its teachings. One can never outgrow his need for purposeful Bible study. Knowledge of its contents provides wisdom for all life's situations. Without such knowledge, a person can be deceived by the enemy of his soul, the devil. There are countless other comments I could make in support of Bible study, but it's time to move on to our topic."

Weeda had begun to squirm. Though the students' jaws were hanging ajar and the proverbial dropping of a pin would have made a sound, she feared Kyle was talking over their heads. How she wished he had run all this by her before today, but there had been no such opportunity. The Houstons had taken up every smidgen of their off-duty time. While observing the reactions of the group and

with these little negatives racing through her mind, she saw
Hammie Hanks looking completely absorbed with what Kyle was
saying, so she reasoned that if Kyle were registering with Hammie,
surely there was no need to worry about the other forty-nine. When
she turned her attention back to Kyle, he was still in his lecture
mode.

"Before I delve into our question for today, let me make a suggestion. Don't argue with people about the age of the earth or the age of
unearthed fossils. If the archaeologists are right about their claims,
they're right; if they're wrong, they're wrong. Their claims, right or
wrong, won't contradict the Bible because the Bible doesn't set time
limits concerning the existence of the pre-Adamic earth—that is, the
earth that predates the time of Adam. I see some bewilderment on a
few faces, so I'll make a restatement and try to clarify. Yes, from several passages of Scripture, we can deduce that there was an earth
prior to the one on which you and I live."

Weeda was thinking again that he needed to be less formal, but
she had to admit they were listening. In fact, they appeared spell-
bound. Kyle continued to lecture.

"Sometime in the dateless past God created the heavens and the
earth. According to Genesis 1, verses 1 and 2, the earth was reduced
to a formless and useless mass, probably as the result of a judgment
from God for the sin that infested the planet through Lucifer. The
raw material still existed, but it had been made shapeless, void, and
empty. In the Hebrew, we say it was Tohu, meaning shapeless, and
Bohu, meaning empty. Let me repeat. Both the creation and later the
destruction of the pre-Adamic earth took place in the dateless past;
therefore, the story of creation given to us in the book of Genesis is
really an account of God's taking the formless matter and reforming
it into the earth on which He later created Adam and Eve.

"In making these assertions and in taking this position, scholars
admit to some speculations, but the speculations are not without
foundation. On the handouts we gave you you'll find scripture passages that support these claims and provide the basis for these
assumptions. These references are taken from Isaiah 24, Eziekel 28,
Jeremiah 4, and 2 Peter 3. Later we'll read and discuss some of these
passages. From these passages, you'll glean insights into the person
and nature of Lucifer who, scholars believe, was the overseer of the
earth during this pre-Adamic Age. He ruled until iniquity entered
into him, causing him through pride and ambition to rebel. This
revolt cost him his position in the government of God and brought

about the devastation of the province over which he had ruled. This fallen personality lost his Luciferian title and was renamed Satan.

"How long the pre-Adamic world was in existence we do not know, but we do know that when God restored the earth, He put his newly created man Adam in charge, not Lucifer, who had lost not only his title but also his position. In fact, when he appeared to Eve in the Garden of Eden, he was a trespasser. As you know, first Eve and then Adam bought his lies, and in so doing, Adam lost his right to serve as God's deputy in the earth. Adam's loss was Satan's gain. Here I want to emphasize that Satan's rulership was and still is limited to the earth's social order. The planet, the real estate, belongs to God, and I'm glad to add that all the people who reject Satan and receive Jesus as Lord also belong to God, but only those people who willingly surrender their lives to Jesus are able to come out from under Satan's rulership. This switching is referred to by different terms which all mean very much the same thing. Some people call the experience the 'rebirth' or being 'born again.' Others refer to it as being 'saved' or being 'converted.' Regardless of the reference used, the switching means a person has been transferred from the kingdom of Satan into the Kingdom of God. Well, I'm getting ahead of myself. Let me get back on track.

"As to the beings over which Lucifer ruled, we cannot speak with certainty. Probably there were various orders of beings such as angels, and there could have been human primates whose remains were fossilized and when unearthed today are categorized as prehistoric men. It's unlikely that these primates were on the same level as the human primates of today, which we know scientifically as Homo sapiens. Likely they were the highest-ranking order in the animal kingdom of that age, but they probably did not have a soul. I base that assumption on the fact that in the Genesis account God specialized in making a being in his own image, and in so doing, elevated that primate above other primates by breathing into this created being his very own breath, wherein man, having been made in the image of God, became a living soul.

"Now let's look at certain passages which give us insight into Lucifer's past and into his nature, both before and after his rebellion against God. Take your Bibles and turn to Isaiah 14:12 and following. I'm reading from the King James version. We'll start with verse 12."

How art thou fallen from heaven, O Lucifer, son of the morning! How art thou cut down to the ground, who dids't weaken the

nations! For thou hast said in thine heart, I will ascend into heaven,
I will exalt my throne above the stars of God; I will sit also upon the
mount of the congregation, in the sides of the north, I will ascend
above the heights of the clouds, I will be like the Most High. Yet thou
shall be brought down to sheol, to the sides of the pit. They that see
thee shall narrowly look upon thee, and consider thee, saying, "Is
this the man who made the earth to tremble, who did shake king-
doms, Who made the world like a wilderness, and destroyed its
cities, who opened not the house of his prisoners?"

"These verses tell us that Lucifer, now known as Satan, is to be
judged. His destiny is foretold. If you sometimes wonder about the
terrible destructive forces in the earth, you need wonder no longer.
Satan is the source of much evil. The power he has over the earth's
social order and physical forces is evident in these words. Millions
of people have never cancelled out his ultimate power over them by
surrendering to Christ; therefore, much of our society has never
been released from his influence, and he uses unbelievers and those
who discount his existence to keep his will in motion. Of course, his
power is limited, but he can exercise enough to make war, to promote diseases and to harass Christians and weaken their testimony
for Christ.

"Now turn in your Bibles to Ezekiel 28, verse 12b and follow
along as I read through verse 19."

Thus saith the Lord God: Thou sealest up the sum, full of wis-
dom, and perfect in beauty. Thou has been in Eden, the garden, O
God; every precious stone was thy covering, the sardius, topaz, and
the diamond, the beryl, the onyx, and the jasper, the sapphire, the
emerald, and the carbuncle, and gold; the workmanship of thy tim-
brels and of thy flutes was prepared in thee in the day that thou wast
created. Thou art the anointed cherub that covereth, and I have set
thee so; thou wast upon the holy mountain of God; thou hast walked
up and down in the midst of the stones of fire. Thou was perfect in
thy ways from the day that thou wast created, till iniquity was
found in thee. By the multitude of thy merchandise they have filled
the midst of thee with violence, and hast sinned; therefore, I will cast
thee as profane out of the mountain of God, and I will destroy thee,
O covering cherub, from the midst of the stones of fire. Thine heart
was lifted up because of thy beauty; thou hast corrupted thy wisdom
by reason of thy brightness; I will cast thee to the ground, I will lay

thee before kings, that they may behold thee. Thou hast defiled thy sanctuaries by the multitude of thine iniquities, by the iniquity of thy merchandise; therefore will I bring forth a fire from the midst of thee; it shall devour thee, and I will bring thee to ashes upon the earth in the sight of all them that behold thee. All they that know thee among the people shall be appalled at thee; thou shalt be a terror, and never shalt thou be any more.

"From these Scriptures, we learn much about the one we sometimes refer to as the devil. We see that he once was a part of the mountain of God—mountain is a synonym, another name, for the government of God. His merchandising, the promotion of greed among people and among nations, accounts for much strife and fighting in the earth, and he was thrown out because iniquities were found in him. Also, we see as we did in Isaiah that God will bring Satan's power and terror to an end.

"I'm getting a signal from Mr. Bryant that it's time for a break. I understand there are refreshments in the grill—fruit punch and apple chips—no junk food so close to lunchtime. We'll reassemble here in twenty minutes and spend some time answering questions related to these passages and also to the topic of creation. See you at 11:30."

* * *

The students filed back into the chapel on schedule, and Kyle answered their questions, most of which were related to the Genesis story of creation. At twelve Mr. Bryant dismissed the group and left for an appointment, leaving Weeda and Kyle to check for any clutter or personal items left behind. Almost immediately, Weeda offered her assessment.

"Kyle, it went over really well. At first, I was afraid you might be over their heads, but not so; they were attentive throughout. I wish I had made a tape. There are a few professional teachers who could learn a thing or two from you."

"Thanks, but it wasn't the technique, the method, or the teacher, but the subject matter. God anoints His word. Regardless of the styles or methods of presentation, the Holy Spirit highlights God's truths so people will be drawn to it, and that's as it should be. The focus is on the message, not the messenger."

"Well put. I'm so glad it went so well. I'll look forward to being here again two weeks from today for another study."

As they approached the exit and before he could make a response, someone from the outside opened the door, and a familiar-looking young male appeared. There they stood face to face with Sonny Houston.

Kyle seemed unmoved, but Weeda was discombobulated. He was in army fatigues, disheveled, thin. She needed convincing that the tall lanky lad was who she thought he was.

"Are you—are you? Yes, you are. Wh-what are you doing here, Sonny?"

"I can't...can we get out of the door? Move inside?"

Kyle, quickly glancing around outside for he didn't know what, said, "Come on in. Are you running, hiding?"

"Both. Running and hiding."

"From what—I mean who?"

"I don't know how to tell you."

As they took seats around the small reception table in the narthex, Kyle and Weeda exchanged knowing yet questioning looks of suspicion, and Kyle started some questioning.

"Fill us in, Sonny. What's this all about?"

"I wanted to see Ms. McVey and hoped she would still be here. When I talked to Macy last she told me the Bible Club would be meeting here this morning, so I waited 'til everybody was gone."

"Did somebody drop you off? When I glanced outside, I saw only two cars—mine and Ms. McVey's."

"I'm on my motor bike. It's in the bushes."

"In the bushes? That's odd. Who're you hiding from?"

"From the other twelve."

Kyle gave Weeda another knowing look. "What other twelve? Are you telling me you're in a group made up of thirteen members? Is that what you're saying?"

"That's what I'm saying."

"Are you part of a coven?"

"That's what some people call it, I suppose." He started shaking and with broken speech continued. "I want out, but they won't let me. They'll kill me before they'll let me out."

"So that explains the army fatigues and the hidden bike?"

He nodded. "The others are on a special assignment this weekend."

Weeda butted in. "But Sonny, when and how did you get mixed up with something like this? When?"

"Soon after I talked to you about the adoption. I was so mixed up, and a guy from another school told me how I could get all my questions answered and things turned around through a psychic. So I started out with psychic readings and numerology, and that led to other things. They said I advanced so rapidly that they recommended me for special assignments."

"What special assignment?"

"I'd better not say. It was exciting for a while, but last weekend I had my eyes opened, too late. I was already in and they won't let me out, and besides, I'm hooked. Only a part of me wants out. Something inside, telling me things, directing me."

Kyle reacted. "I assume this thing is not very active now?"

"You're right. Otherwise, I wouldn't be telling you these things."

"That's what I'm getting at. Be specific. What does your guide tell you to do?"

"I'd better not say."

"Does it entice you to be dangerous in any way?"

Sonny's body went rigid, his eyes slitted, and his teeth started grinding. The hatred from his eyes toward the two of them brought a gasp from Weeda that she tried to stifle. Kyle countered with, "In the name of Jesus I bind you, you wicked spirit of violence. I command you to cease and desist."

Immediately, Sonny's expression changed, his features softened, and his pupils retracted. When he regained control, he said, "I want out. I need help. Where can I get help?"

"Do your parents know where you are?"

"No, they think I'm in my room. I left through a window."

Feigning ignorance, Kyle probed further. "Are you on good terms with your parents?"

"No, not at all, but I got a letter from Dad in the mail this morning."

"A letter?"

He nodded. "After I read it, I was determined to get out." Weeda was dumbfounded. Thank goodness, Kyle was in charge! She was not able to do anything but gawk in disbelief.

"You say the letter made you more determined to get free?"

"It was his confession about my adoption, which was pure bosh. He didn't adopt me. He's my read dad, and Sally, his secretary, was my real mom. He asked me to forgive him. It was about ten pages long."

"Will you forgive him, or have you already done so?"

"Right now I think I have, and when I read it, I thought I had, but when my guide takes over, I can't forgive."

"Explain. What does your guide advise?"

"It tells me all the reasons why Dad doesn't deserve forgiveness and why I shouldn't communicate with him and all that."

"How else does he guide and direct?"

"Explains how I can advance more rapidly by bringing someone's life to an end."

"Does he give you a plan to carry this out?"

"Sure thing, and it's lock-safe. Nobody would ever be able to figure out how it happened or who did it."

"You want to share the plan?"

Shrugging his shoulders, he said, "No way!"

Kyle spoke to the demon again, settling it back down, and Sonny continued with additional revelations.

"If I do away with somebody, I'll be rewarded with certain powers and wisdom. I'll be able to determine my own destiny and can become whatever I want to become. No special effort on my part required."

"Sonny, you grew up as a Christian, didn't you?"

He stiffened again. "That's what I was told."

"What about now? What are your thoughts?"

"It's gone. I don't wanta say—I can't say certain things."

"You can't call on Jesus—can't say that name?" Sonny nodded. "Not even now?"

"Not even now."

"You said you had your eyes opened last weekend. What happened to bring that about?"

"I can't say," but drawing his index finger across his throat, he gave the slashing sign.

"When you were sworn in as a member, were you required to renounce Christianity?"

"Renounce? I think so. Yeah! I know so."

The three sat silently for a minute. Though the dialogue had slowed down, Kyle's mental processes were racing in all directions, trying to figure out just what to do next. He pursed his lips then let out a long sigh—a sign of perplexed thinking "Sonny, you're in a heap-o-trouble, and you need to understand that it'll take determination and a deliberate effort to get free. But it can be done, and the sooner you start, the better."

"Right now, I'm willing, but how?"

"How do they stay in touch with you?"

"By phone. Nearly all arrangements are made by phone. Most messages are coded."

"OK. Be sure things stay that way. Continue to play ball with them. Continue to receive their messages and instructions as you've been doing, but you're going to be unable to attend any meetings or fulfill any assignments. You'll be ill—at home, sick, unable to attend school. Do you understand?"

"I hear you. I've already told my folks I won't be going to school, but they don't know why. They don't know I've switched my religion. They just can't figure out why I won't go to church anymore. Just like at school. They don't know what's going on."

Kyle looked at Weeda. "You deal with the school, OK?"

She was pensive and reluctant but nodded affirmatively.

"I'll talk to the parents."

"What will you tell them?" asked Sonny.

"I'll level with them and explain why it's best for you to stay out of school for the time being. I'll verify your illness, and I won't have to alter the truth. You are sick, very sick, with a condition affecting your body, your soul, and your spirit."

"What about my guide? He'll have something to say about all this."

"That's a lie he wants you to believe. Rest assured: Jesus can set you free, but sometimes in these kinds of involvements, it takes time, patience, and much intercession to loosen Satan's tentacles. You've given him some strong legal rights to your soul, and he doesn't give up without a fight. Your guide knows about these decisions, so in the name of Jesus I bind that demon and cancel out his ability to serve as an informer against you. In that way, the coven will continue to deal with you but without any assistance from the guide. At first, they'll very likely accept your explanation of sickness without questioning. That'll give us time to seek the Lord and get organized for a spiritual offensive. Hopefully, by the time they know for sure that you're pulling out, we'll have some spiritual warfare adequately organized to deal with them."

Skepticism clouded Sonny's face and he shook his head in doubt. "They're powerful. I hope you're right about your power source. As much as I want help, I'm warning you. They know how to get what they want, and when they want more power, they make a sacrifice. That's why they want me to kill, and the scary thing is that there are times when I want to cooperate with them to get more power."

The three sat silent again. Though the dialogue had ceased, Kyle's mental faculties had shifted into overdrive. He sent up a quick prayer, asking the Lord for direction. Suddenly, the foyer door opened and in walked a uniformed gentleman. He apologized for the intrusion then asked if the motorbike in the shrubbery belonged to anybody they knew. Sonny explained, saying he had misplaced the bike's lock so he had tried to hide it to prevent theft. The officer accepted the explanation and left, cautioning Sonny to try doing a better hiding job next time.

As the officer was leaving, Sonny excused himself to go to the restroom. As soon as he was out of hearing, Kyle explained that he thought the officer was Cody's detective, checking up on Sonny.

"How do you know that?"

"I've seen the man around the med complex from time to time, and I know what he does."

"Well, I'm glad he's on the job. If Sonny is being covered so well, why can't he return to school?"

"You're forgetting the strategy, my dear. Sonny will be too sick to attend school, remember? He thinks he's being watched, and he might be right."

"Kyle, I suppose I've become a go-between. Mr. Drago has asked school personnel to be on the lookout for signs of occult involvement, saying police have warned superintendents about such activities in the area, but since we're a Christian school, I was hoping we wouldn't have too much reason to be concerned. I'm astounded, but this explains Sonny's strange phone calls and all that. We both suspected drugs, but not this."

"So often the two go together. So tragic. Deliverance doesn't always come easy. I've observed two such sessions with the Corleys. Even after the victims are free from their beliefs and practices, some carry wounds that are slow to heal, and the healing leaves scars, making them vulnerable in various ways. There's a high price to pay when one actively and deliberately pledges allegiance to Satan and spends time on his turf."

"Sonny's taking his time."

"Yeah. He's probably not wanting to face up, and I can't say I'm looking forward to any involvement. Except for writing his medical excuses, I'll have to leave all the arrangements to you. I have an unusually heavy schedule next week, but I will call the Corleys to let them know they have a client wanting release from the Satanists in the area. They'll give priority to the case because they want so much to see the devil lose his hold on some of the local young people."

"What about Cody? He has to be informed."

"Right. I'll call you later this afternoon after I've talked to him, or better still, why don't I pick you up around six and we'll have dinner at Westwinds?"

"Sure, that's fine, but right now I'm thinking it'll be Monday before I can talk to Drago. Here comes Sonny."

"I was about to come looking for you," said Kyle. "Never mind taking a seat. We have to be on our way. If it'll make you feel better, I'll follow you home, and Ms. McVey will be in touch with you. Remember, you're to stay at home and wait to hear from her."

* * *

Shortly after six, Kyle and Weeda were on the road to Westwinds. "Kyle, I can't believe we're together for what I hope will be a bit of a respite. It's been so long since we had an evening to ourselves."

"You're right, but I'm afraid we won't be totally alone tonight."

"What do you mean? Somebody joining us?"

"Nobody in person, I hope, but certain clients will still dominate our time, that is, our thoughts and interests. I did talk to Cody and also to the Corleys this afternoon."

"I can't wait to hear their reactions. In fact, I wanted to call you, but I knew you were probably getting dressed and I didn't want to delay our dinner."

"For now, I'll just say he and Anna were stunned and confused but relieved that there's the possibility of a solution. Here's the restaurant. I'll tell you more after we've ordered. I'm hungry, and I hope you are too."

After ordering light appetizers and seafood platters, Weeda started asking questions. "How did you approach Cody?"

"To start with, he was not aware that Sonny had been away from home this afternoon, not until the detective called and informed him that he was with us. Cody was encouraged by that, taking it as a signal that the boy was having a change of heart and was getting help from us. He couldn't receive what I told him about Sonny's involvement in devil worship. He couldn't accept the concept."

"I'm not surprised. How much did he understand?"

"Very little. He doesn't accept the reality of a personal devil, so in his mind, Sonny's freedom is just a simple matter of disassociating himself from the wackos who are playing fantasy games. As with many Christians, there are gaps in his spiritual reasoning. He rejoices that he's saved but apparently has never considered or questioned what he has been saved from. The man has spent hours in the congregation facing the pulpit. How did he escape learning some basic fundamentals?"

"But Kyle, the fundamentals you have in mind are sometimes hard to come by. Much of the trouble lies in the churches themselves. They teach a social gospel that avoids dealing with the unpleasant realities of sin, Satan, and hell. Even so, we must keep in mind that Cody has been playing church, and even had he been exposed to teachings covering the whole counsel of God, it's unlikely his mind registered what his ears were exposed to."

"That's true. But I'm thinking not only of Cody's biblical ignorance but about many Christians in general. In my work, I'm constantly seeing people who are church-oriented but not Christ-oriented. They promote the church but have little regard for what Jesus actually proclaimed."

She nodded in agreement. "Even trained ordained ministers attempt to sanitize what Jesus taught, trying to make the message palatable for today's cultivated churchgoers. That's one of the reasons the Cody Houstons know little or nothing about Satan, hell, or the demonic world."

"Yeah, and they dress wrongdoings up in all kind of euphemisms so that sinful actions become acceptable behaviors—aberrations, maladjustments."

"I'm agreeing. See, I've begun to take on your viewpoints. You're right about Cody."

"Don't think I haven't noticed the stances you're taking these days. It's delightful to have a meeting of minds. Back to Cody, I'm not implying he is in denial because he doesn't know the truth to deny it. His problem is ignorance. He thinks Sonny's playing a game, and all he has to do to get himself straight is to quit the game as one would give up soccer or baseball. I realized I was up against a brick wall trying to explain deliverance to him, so I started talking in terms of counseling, something he could relate to. I suggested his getting help from the Corleys. He wasn't agreeable at first, wanting you and me to tackle the job, an undertaking I'm not yet qualified to tackle."

"I don't know that I agree with you there, but his request figures. He wants us to do the job so he can keep the whole can of worms confined to as few people as possible."

"Even if I felt confident about the task, my work load is too heavy to take on such an assignment; however, I am willing to arrange and facilitate where I can."

"Ditto! I'd be at a loss about where and how to deal with something that powerful. There are some case studies on demonology in that last book you gave me, but I haven't gotten to them yet. I suppose I should so I'll know what Sonny and the Corleys are in for."

"Good, and I think it would be wise if you sat in on these sessions."

"You can't be serious?"

"I am serious. You could back them up in prayer, and besides, it would give you an opportunity to learn the procedures. Trust me; it'll turn out to be a blessing."

"Something like what I experienced?"

"Right. The difference is a matter of degree and emphasis. For you the emphasis was remorse followed by forgiveness. With Sonny, much of the effort will very likely focus on remorse followed by renunciation. The Corleys are asking for concerted prayer—organized intercession to break Satan's power."

"Did they give you a time line?"

"No, first they want to make some arrangements with a minister here in Rushton, someone they have worked with previously who has been instrumental in helping youth break free from occultism."

"Really? From what church?"

"I jotted it all down. Here it is on my pocket notepad. He is Pastor Hilton Savage from Hilltop Community Church."

"Hilltop? We have a few students who attend there. I'm not sure what denomination they are."

"Corley says the church is interdenominational and that this pastor is very strong in doing spiritual warfare and is especially interested in ministering to youth."

"Wow! Is that a blessing or what?"

"Yeah! And that's another reason you'd be smart to sit in on these sessions. You'd get to know the man."

"True. Sounds like a good resource person for our school." She became quiet and pensive, lost in thought. "Kyle, I look back and I can't believe it. One counselee, Sonny Houston and his problem, has been indirectly responsible for leading me from a nominal Christian stance to one of, well, I don't know how to say it. I know I've grown as a believer, but I also feel I've been led from Point A not quite to Point Z but very close—maybe Point X, and pardon the pun, but I'll be glad to take an X-it after I've seen victory for that family. I'm not making sense, but I will do whatever I can wherever I can, so if sitting in will help, I'll do it. I could never have come this far without your help. Our sharing has definitely been one-sided and in my favor. About the only help I've been able to offer you has been through prayer. I'm still praying for Lola, the woman who suffered from post-abortion syndrome. The other night you said you were encouraged about her."

"I am. She is still making confessions, and it's making a difference. I'm reducing her anti-depressant, and she's sleeping at night. Also, she's being reconciled with her husband. I can't emphasize it enough: Some of the best curative agents for the ills of humanity don't come in capsules and pills but in the forgiving love of Jesus Christ, and Lola is learning that. She is a prime example of a Christian whose redeemed spirit was trying to convince her deceived mind to confess and repent. The struggle between the two had made her a classic neurotic."

"I'm beginning to understand those things. In fact, I'm learning that the practice of Christianity is a 24/7 occupation."

"You're right, and I'm very much aware that you and I haven't had time to promote our own relationship. Have you noticed?"

"Have I noticed? So much so that I stay in a constant state of resentment, and you'd probably classify that resentment as a sin in itself, yes?"

He laughed. "Maybe so, but now that you've made a confession, we'll pronounce forgiveness and see what we can do to remedy the situation."

"What do you have in mind? Anything definite?"

"Well, for a starter, when my next free weekend comes up, we could spend the time together at home with my parents."

"I'd like that. I won't let you forget."

"I won't need reminding. I'll let Mom know and she'll be in touch with you and extend an invitation. Back to the Corleys. I gave them your phone number, so they'll be calling concerning Sonny's appointment. That'll be after they've made arrangements to get the minister involved and all that."

"I need to jot down all these 'to do' things. First, I must inform Drago and enlist his aid." She continued writing as Kyle kept instructing.

"I forgot to tell you that Corley is bringing or sending you a few copies of a book on spiritual warfare. He'd like you to distribute them to the intercessors and suggests giving Cody a copy. Maybe Mr. Drago would like one."

"What about you—one for you?"

"Not necessarily. I'll read yours later. I've read a few books on the subject but not this particular one. Also, when you talk to your principal, you might get approval to set up Sonny's appointment during school hours. On second thought, that won't be necessary since he'll be out of school anyway. The Corleys made that suggestion because they're trying to keep the weekends for themselves. Drago won't object to your being away for those sessions, will he?"

"I don't think so since I'll be involved in an unusual type of counseling, won't I?"

"To say the least. One of the things that concerns me most is the probability that Sonny will vacillate—on again, off again. When those spirits realize Sonny means business and is defecting, they might pressure him to become dangerous. We should give Cody some warnings. Hopefully, he will compute the seriousness of what they're all up against."

"'Uncharted waters'! Think I'll label Sonny's file under that name."

"Appropriate. She's bringing the check. It's not really late, so if it's OK, why don't we pray about all these things when we get to your place, and if the Lord's willing, we'll spend some time promoting our own personal relationship."

"Needless to say, I'm ready for that. This has been one busy Saturday."

* * *

The following Monday afternoon Weeda drove home from school exhausted. The day had been too full. She had talked at length with the principal, explaining Sonny's troubles and absences. She had briefly counseled with five different students and then talked back and forth with Cody and the Corleys. At three o'clock a faculty meeting was called, which extended the day by another hour. She had not had any direct contact with Sonny but suspected by what Cody had said that he was vacillating, just as Kyle had predicted, going back and forth from cooperation to rebellion.

Still mulling over her conversations of the day, she entered the house, plopped her handbag and briefcase down on the coffee table and was just about to sprawl out on the sofa when the blinking light on the answering machine caught her eye. It was a message from Kyle: "It's about four o'clock. I should be finished with my rounds by seven. I'll pick up some steaks at the Flame Pit and be at your place about eight. Call and leave a yes or no message on my home machine. Hope to see you then." Not up to preparing a meal and too tired to eat out, she was more than pleased. She put a yes message on his machine, stretched out on the sofa, and promptly fell asleep.

Kyle arrived shortly before eight. Being hungry, they both ate with gusto the to-go meal of steaks, baked potato, tossed salad, and garlic bread, and while doing so reported on the activities and arrangements each had made during the day.

"Kyle, God is surely working in this situation. I was relieved that Drago received the news about Sonny in the spirit he did. He knew the boy was in deep trouble, but like us he had suspected drugs. He is more than willing to cooperate with the minister, but, of course, he is required to report the basic facts of all this to the county officials. He offered the school facilities for the Corley session."

"Did you relay that offer to them?"

"I did, but they said they preferred to work on their own turf. I was surprised that he knew so much about deliverance, but he didn't go into any details. He just said he knew of cases where such procedures had made all the difference in people's lives."

"I'm impressed. What about Cody? How did you come out with him and Anna? I hope he's realizing how serious the situation is."

"I think so. Just as you predicted, Sonny is vacillating and that has Cody concerned. For instance, Sonny expressed his forgiveness, and Cody took that as a sure sign that reconciliation was for sure, but later he left a note at Cody's place on the dinette table."

"Not good, I presume."

"I wrote it down in my notes. It went something to this effect: 'I can't let you off so easy. You must pay for what you have done. You will know and understand the exact penalty and the price when the time is right.'"

"I hope you warned Cody about the implication of such a message."

"I tried to. I explained how these occult members can be danger-ous, especially when the devil realizes one of his members is about to defect."

"Could he receive that?"

"I hope so. Drago, Pastor Savage, and the Corleys are meeting Tuesday night at Savage's church to do what the Corleys call spiritu-al warfare. Drago says he will insist that Cody and Anna attend."

"Good, that should open Cody's eyes to some truths not often taught."

"Can you attend?"

"No way. Our group is sponsoring a seminar, and I'll have to be on hand, but I'll be waiting for a report. It might be wise to phone Sonny from time to time just to make sure he isn't trying to pull off something—bowing out or getting lost. And when you talk to Cody, find out if he is keeping the private detective advised about what's going on just in case."

"Oh! I forgot to tell you. Cody released the detective—didn't think he needed his services since the boy is now staying at home."

"Well, that settles that. I'll help you clear the table and I'll scoot."

"That's not necessary. You cooked; I'll clean up. With a delivered meal like this, there's very little to do afterwards."

"If you insist. I do have that seminar and I'm running short on time." He gave her a quick hug, saying, "Keep praying and keep me updated."

As he rushed toward the car, he added, "And if you get to the prayer meeting, be sure to fill me in on how it goes."

* * *

Weeda did attend the prayer meeting at Hilltop on Tuesday evening and at eleven o'clock that night was looking over the notes she had made for Kyle's benefit. He had asked for an account, and she knew she wouldn't remember the details unless she jotted them down. Though the content was abbreviated, she had taken the time after reaching home to outline her notes and make a few personal observations. Because he was seeing patients all day and attending the seminar in the evenings, she probably wouldn't see him before the weekend. Perhaps it would be smart to drop it off at his place on her way to work in the morning. That way, they'd have a point of ref-erence if, by chance, they had the need to discuss anything by phone. She rapidly rechecked her notes:

Tuesday Evening Prayer Meeting Hilltop Community Church

7:30 p.m.
Pastor introduced the 14 attendees, Stated Purpose: To break up occult group, headquartered within 3-county area. Recruiting tactics: Prey on youth with personal problems—start out helpfully, then slowly graduate to sinister tactics. Ultimate goal: to have members renounce Christianity and pledge loyalty to Satan.
(Personal Observation: Cody was fidgety but attentive. I was fidgety too but enlightened.)

8:00 p.m.
Corley talked: Focused on prayer as means of bringing Sonny into freedom. Passed out copies of PRAYER TO BREAK BONDAGE (Copy attached) and dealt briefly with each suggestion. (Very good.) Discussed upcoming sessions.
(Personal Observation: Cody uttered "Amen." Glad to hear it. Had noticed negative facial expressions. Anna was silent but attentive, patting Cody on knee from X to X.)
Emphasized need to pray that Sonny will retain desire to defect, Sonny will cooperate with counselors, school personnel, and all in authority. People involved (prayer warriors, family members, counselors) will be protected from all harm, all related efforts and events be under auspices of Holy Spirit.

8:30 p.m.
Group, led by Savage, prayed according to outline (powerful) followed by concerted prayer—lasted half hour.

9:00 p.m.
Questions and Answers (directed by Savage and Corley)
Q: Since Sonny is focus, why is he not here?
A: Sonny not aware these steps being made in his behalf. At this stage, not certain of his full commitment. Firm foundation of prayer and faith needed to deal with devilish involvements.
Q: How and when will Sonny become involved?
A: For the past few days, Sonny has agreed to go for intensive help from the Corleys. If all goes according to plans, counseling will begin Friday of this week.
Q: Will this prayer group remain the same as to number, etc.?

A: For the time being, yes. You were enlisted as people who understand the need for intercession. Many Christians do not accept the reality of a satanic world, and through unbelief are hindrances, not help.

Q: How often will we meet?

A: Some of us will meet nightly until victory comes. There are 16 of us. Two could not be here tonight. Meeting in prayer room will not interfere with other church functions.

Addendum: Kyle, on Friday, I'm riding down to Dellisville with Pastor Savage and two ladies on the prayer team. Cody will be driving Sonny and Anna down. Session starts at ten. Know you'll be busy, but maybe we can talk Friday night.

* * *

It had been a long day for Weeda. The ride to and from Dellisville, the waiting, the praying, and the phone contacts afterwards had left her depleted. Now she was waiting for Kyle to call so she could relay to him the day's frustrations, the disappointments, and get his advice. In spite of the inner turmoil, fatigue took over and she fell asleep on the sofa—a deep slumber from which she did not stir until the phone rang shortly before eight. Immediately, she was alert at the sound of Kyle's voice.

"Hi Weeda, I've been anxious for a report but haven't had an opportunity to call."

"Kyle, you won't believe what happened."

"Yes, I will. You forget I believe in the power of God to perform."

"I wish it were so, but that's not what happened."

"Oh?"

"Nothing happened. The Houstons and Sonny did not show up."

"Didn't show up? Are you saying they stood you people up?"

"That's right. No calls or explanation or anything. Pastor Savage made calls to Cody's house but nobody answered. They're afraid there's been some foul play, but they don't want to be alarmists."

"Sounds like tactics of the devil to thwart God's purposes. Did they call Houston Enterprises?"

"They did, and the secretary, not knowing anything about the Dellisville trip, said the Houstons have taken off two weeks for personal and family reasons, and she was not concerned. Said they had given the maid time off too. She felt sure they had gone away for the weekend and would likely touch base soon. Said he always stayed in touch when he was out of town. Knowing how guarded Cody is about what's going on, nothing was mentioned to the secretary about the counseling sessions."

"That's good reasoning assuming there's nothing wrong except a change of mind—cold feet—but something's not adding up. Surely Cody would have called you or the Corleys to cancel. A flag went up with me when I read your note about the riding arrangements, but in a rush, I disregarded the signal."

"That's understandable, considering all the demands being made on you."

"Did anybody have Cody's cell phone number?"

"I did, and I called both his and Sonny's number but no answer."

"Wait and see, I suppose, but this is alarming."

"I know. I talked with Corley just before I fell asleep. He said he'd continue to wait but come morning he felt he had no choice but to inform authorities about these odd circumstances. I urged him to be discreet. I don't think he or Savage is yet aware of the thorny adoption issue. That'll no doubt surface during the session if and when such comes to pass."

"That's smart. Since the appointment was broken with the Corleys, it's their responsibility to deal with the no show."

"Thanks, Kyle. That's how I see it. Pastor Savage has the prayer team interceding at the church. The members are praying in shifts around the clock until they have a breakthrough or at least get a release from the burden."

"Good. I would go down and join them, but I'll be in the seminar until ten; then I have to look in on some hospital patients. But beep me if you find out anything, and I'll manage to give you a ring."

"That I will do."

* * *

At six the next morning Weeda was awake, wondering if anybody had heard anything. Apparently not since she had not been called. It was too early to disturb Pastor Savage or the Corleys, but she was anxious. She reasoned that if she had not heard anything by seven then she would make some calls. Suddenly it occurred to her that somebody in the prayer room might know something, so she called that number.

"The prayer room, Hilltop Church, Bill Dozier speaking."

"Yes, this is Weeda McVey. You probably don't remember me. I was at the organizational prayer meeting the other evening."

"Sure. The counselor from the Christian school."

"Right. I'm trying to get in touch with Pastor Savage. Is he there?"

"No, he left about an hour ago, saying he'd be back later. He has us praying without ceasing. We don't know the details, just that the situation is serious. God knows the circumstances, and we're believing for His will to be done. And I might add that we're expecting something to happen soon."

"I'll agree to that. Thank you very much."

She hung up, disappointed that she had not learned anything. Oh well, she thought, I might as well have some breakfast; then I'll give myself over to prayer.

Just as she was finishing her oatmeal and toast, the phone rang.

"Hello?"

"Ms. McVey, this is Cody Houston."

She almost dropped the phone but managed to say, "Cody Houston, thank God! Are you all right? Are Sonny and Anna all right?"

"We hope we're out of danger now, but it's been an ordeal."

"Where are you and what happened?"

"I hated to bother you, but..."

"Go ahead. I'm so relieved to hear from you."

"We're in Dellisville Motel—been holed up here since we reached town yesterday morning. Sonny reneged, threatened suicide and had a gun to carry out his threat unless we met his demand to check in a motel and give him time to rethink. Well, we've been through hell all night. About an hour ago, Sonny's resistance broke down. He gave Anna the gun and has been crying and begging the Lord to forgive him."

"How horrible, but how wonderful for the change. Are you headed back to Rushton?"

"That's what we're trying to decide. We need direction. Sonny's in such a state. He's hoping the Corleys might be able to help him while we're here. Could you approach them to find out?"

"That would be great. I'll do my best to find out. Can you stay where you are while I make some calls. Are you safe and all that?"

"We are now. Sonny turned the gun over to Anna. She took it somewhere, just where I didn't ask. Check-out time is eleven. Sonny wants to talk to somebody about Jesus."

"Well, praise the Lord! Give me the phone number at the motel, and your room number. I'll get back to you as soon as I find out something."

* * *

An hour later, Weeda rang Cody's room number.

"Hello."

"Mr. Houston, This is Weeda McVey. I've made some arrangements. Sonny still wanting help, I hope?"

"So far. He's getting impatient."

"Good. That means he's more likely to cooperate. The Corleys made some changes in their plans for the day just so they can see Sonny this morning. You have the directions to their place?"

"Yes. We drove by there yesterday. That's when the boy got cold feet and backed out."

"Well, let's pray he'll stay the course today. Try to be there no later than 10:30. Pastor Savage is on his way and will probably be there by that time. The prayer team will remain praying at the church here. There's a place at the center where you and Anna can wait and intercede."

"Thank you. Thank you! I've jotted all this down. Christian Center at 10:30."

"Right. I won't detain you further. I'm believing in faith that Sonny will get some help this morning."

"So am I. Thank you again."

* * *

That afternoon, Kyle joined the intercessors at Hilltop, but Weeda stayed home near the phone in the event the Corleys or Pastor Savage called.

Near evening, Kyle called, saying another prayer shift would be coming in at seven and he'd be leaving. He accepted her invitation to come by for sandwiches and chips so she could continue to stay near the phone. Plus, she needed to tap into his insights and benefit from his advice.

They munched on the sandwiches and drank hot chocolate while rehashing the turn of events. "I can't wait, Kyle, to hear how it went at that session today. Pastor Savage called about eleven saying they were getting started, that Sonny had just finished filling out the papers. He also added that he would sit in on the counseling session, but the Houstons would wait in the prayer room."

"Did Savage mention Sonny's state of mind?"

"Indirectly, that the boy was sobbing and could hardly write. He took that as a sign that he was under conviction."

"Good. That'll make the deliverance easier."

"And more quickly. I thought Savage would have called by now. If he calls while you're here, I suggest you go pick up in my bedroom and join in. Do you suppose they've been in session all day?"

"Could be, and sometimes several sessions are needed. This kind of ministry is fairly new to me, but I understand many Christians who have been involved in the occult need help for months and sometimes years."

"I do hope Sonny won't have any permanent scars."

"I know, but don't be surprised if he does. Fortunately, he hasn't been involved very long. And for that reason, I find it hard to understand how he became entrenched in a coven that quickly."

"Do you think he has been honest about his level of involvement?"

"What he claimed checks out with what I've read, but beyond that I can't say. Hopefully, the Corleys can shed some light and maybe be able to determine from the boy's confessions the strength of the occult group or groups in and around these areas."

"That would really be a breakthrough. Changing the subject, how did the seminar turn out?"

"I think everybody was pleased. Technology sets a fast pace for medical workers, and these organized seminars provide one way for us to stay abreast, so in that respect, seminars are an advantage for people like me who don't especially like to travel long distances for updates."

The telephone rang. Weeda answered and gave Kyle the signal that it was Pastor Savage and pointed to the bedroom.

"Pastor Savage, so glad to hear your voice. What can you tell us? Kyle's on the other phone."

"Things went well. As I told you, he was really under conviction—the result of all the intercession, I'm sure. As was the case in the book of Luke, the Holy Spirit was present to deliver and heal. He renounced all occult connections and pleaded forgiveness, and confessed Jesus as Lord. Victory, glorious victory was evident."

"How wonderful. What was Mr. Houston's reaction?"

"So touching. The Corleys called them into the session during the last fifteen minutes, and you should have seen how the dad and son came together in the Lord, confessing and forgiving. Ms. Houston also joined in. It warmed my heart."

"I can sense that," said Kyle, "and it warms our hearts to hear about it. I suppose there'll be some follow-up?"

"We have no choice but to stay involved, but something very serious has come up since Sonny reached home. That's the reason I'm late calling."

"How serious?"

"Hard to say, but it'll require more and more prayer and no doubt a great of direct involvement."

"Are you free to share, to say what it is?"

"Oh yes. Shortly after Sonny got to his room, he had a call from somebody in the group telling him they were suspicious that he was defecting. Threats were made on his life, emphasizing that the threats would be carried out unless he proved his loyalty right away. To prove that loyalty, they are requiring him to meet them in Sunset Cemetery at a specified area at midnight Wednesday."

"My, my! This is something beyond me," said Kyle.

"Dr. Sanders, you're right. In fact, it's beyond any of us apart from the power of the Holy Spirit. No time to let up now. I'm waiting for the Corleys to call advising me where to go from here. I've dealt with a few cases of devil worship, but this is my first experience with a death threat. Let's all keep Sonny covered in prayer."

"Sure thing, Pastor, and God bless."

About half an hour later while Weeda and Kyle were still in prayer, the telephone rang. It was Pastor Savage again.

"I've been on the phone with the Corleys. They're suggesting a special strategy for dealing with the graveyard situation. I'll present their plan to the intercessors Monday night in the prayer room at seven, and we're counting on you to serve as prayer warriors with us at the cemetery that night."

Kyle was baffled by what he thought he heard and asked for a clarification. "I-I'm not sure I understand. Where will the intercessors be while Sonny goes to the cemetery?"

"I was a bit shocked at the plan myself, but the Corleys know more about this than I do. Yes, the intercessors are to go to the graveyard. I'll explain it fully Monday night. Hate to rush, but I have several calls to make."

"Pastor, I'm not being facetious, but if you want the team to sleep tonight, wait until Monday to present them your strategy."

* * *

On Monday evening, Pastor Savage stood before the intercessors—twelve in all—outlining the plans for Wednesday night.

"By now all of you are aware that as a result of your travail and intercession, Sonny Houston is getting his life turned around after being hooked up with some devil worshipers. Some members of the satanic group are suspicious that Sonny is turning away from them and are making threats against his life. They are demanding that he prove his loyalty by meeting them Wednesday at midnight inside Sunset Cemetery at the southeast corner where the fencerows come together.

"You are also aware that God has used the Corleys as his instruments to deliver this young man from the strongholds Satan has had in his life. Because these two people have such an anointing for this special kind of ministry, I feel we should take their advice in an effort to bring victory and closure. Incidentally, others of our youth in this and surrounding counties have fallen prey to these occult predators. So tonight I'm giving to you the follow-up strategy. Let's be grateful to the Corleys and cooperate with them in every way we can. Our youth are so precious and so vulnerable. Just think how you'd feel if the victim were your son or daughter.

"We'll meet here with the Corleys in the prayer room Wednesday night at ten, leave our cars here and be driven to the cemetery in the church van. We should be there in place by eleven. Our plan is to place ourselves among the double rows of large shrubs that line the fences which come together at the corner of Wisteria Drive and Smilax Lane. Bill Dozier and I scouted out the place yesterday and again last night, so I don't think getting situated will be complicated. We'll wait among those shrubs for the adversaries to appear at midnight. I'm speaking specifically time wise because members of the occult attach great importance to time. It's a part of the art of practicing astrology. They have instructed Sonny to appear exactly at midnight, no sooner, no later, and they'll join him at 12:10, demanding that he identify himself using specific codes and signals.

"I realize this is an unusual assignment, and quite frankly, I'm somewhat jittery about it, even though I'm one of the so-called spearheads of it. But since it's God's work, I think we need not fear. Remember what the Lord told Jehoshaphat when Judah was threatened by the armies of Moab, Ammon, and Mt. Seir: 'The battle is not yours but the Lord's.'

"Perhaps you're wondering what we'll do for an hour while we're waiting. The answer is we'll pray and be guided by the Holy Spirit. I have no way of predicting just what will develop once we're situated nor just what will transpire when they appear, not how many will be involved. Thank the Lord, we'll have the Corleys leading us.

"Another question concerns Sonny. He will not be with us. Neither will his parents. The Corleys feel the family should stay safely sequestered until a measure of victory is reached. Since they have more experience than I do, I certainly respect their advice, and I know the Houstons do too.

"Well, that covers the plan. If you have questions, stay behind, and I'll do the best I can to answer them. Be sure to wear dark clothing. We'll have very small flashlights and folding campstools for each of you. I suggest we not use the flashlights unless we just have to. Last night the street light from Ivy Lane, which intersects Wisteria, provided enough diffused light that we were able to make out shadows and forms. The grounds are smooth and well kept so walking was not a real problem. We have handed out some leaflets listing prayer objectives and also the words to choruses and hymns we might want to sing while we're waiting for the clock to strike midnight. God bless you for coming. I'll see you Wednesday at ten. In the meantime, keep praying."

The prayer warriors filed out quietly, too absorbed with what they had heard to ask questions.

* * *

The intercessors unloaded at the gate nearest to the southeast corner; then Bill Dozier moved the van away from the cemetery and parked it down Ivy Lane. A few minutes later he was making his way through the dark shadows to join the others and was relieved that in walking the distance of almost a block he had not met anyone. What would people think if they saw him entering a cemetery alone at night? The others had walked in together, which he would imagine helped to dispel for them that spooky feeling now creeping over him. He was thankful this endeavor had been cleared with the custodian earlier. He didn't want to be taken for a grave robber.

As he approached the corner where the pastor had led the group, he could hear them softly harmonizing "He is Lord/ He is Lord/ He has risen from the dead/ And He is Lord/ Every knee shall bow/ Every tongue confess/ That Jesus Christ is Lord."

Visibility was severely limited, but as his eyes adjusted, he was able to distinguish the intercessors from the shrubs.

Weaving in and out from Ligustrum to Podocarpus, he unfolded his stool and sat down by none other than the doctor and was touched by the melody in their voices as they sang "His name is wonderful/ His name is wonderful/ His name is wonderful/ Jesus my Lord/ He is the mighty King/ Master of everything/ His name is wonderful/ Jesus my Lord/ He's the great Shepherd/ The Rock of all ages/ Almighty God is He/ Bow down before Him/ Worship and adore Him/ His name is wonderful/ Jesus my Lord."

They repeated the chorus several times, and when it ended, Bill assumed intercession would begin, but instead someone started humming another chorus and soon the group was providing the words: "Faith in the Father/ And faith in the Son/ Faith in the Holy Ghost/ Great things are being done/ Demons are trembling/ And devils are on the run/ With faith in Christ Jesus/ Our battles are won."

After repeating this tune several times, someone started up another—one that was personalized: "Set Sonny's spirit free to worship Thee/ Set his spirit free to praise Thy name/ Let all bondage go/ And let deliverance flow/ Set his spirit free to worship Thee."

He was amazed at how the group knew what to do without being told and whispered to Kyle, "How does everyone know what to do? We weren't told any specifics?"

"Weeda just asked me the same thing. I would venture to say it's a unity made possible by the Holy Spirit. I've experienced that power a few times, but nothing to top this."

Kyle sensed that Weeda was weeping, but when the soft strains of "O the Blood of Jesus" wafted in their direction, she was able to blend her alto voice in perfect harmony. "O the Blood of Jesus/ O the blood of Jesus/ O the blood of Jesus/ It washes white as snow."

Over and over these phrases were repeated but without monotony. In fact, with each repetition, the significance of the blood as the price exacted for the sins of mankind punctured Bill's subconscious, and shame flooded over his conscious mind. Shame for what? He had heard about the Blood all his life. He was ashamed that it had taken an event such as this to bring him to an understanding, a conscious gratitude, for the tradeoff God had made to purchase back the souls of men. He hoped the others had Sonny's plight at heart. He couldn't think of anything but himself and seemed to have no control over what was happening—something from somewhere just kept tumbling down into his thoughts.

Momentarily, he pictured God the Father, God the Son, and God the Holy Spirit seated around a heavenly conference table. The Father was presenting Plan B for the redemption of the earth and of mankind. Plan A, presented through the nation of Israel, had failed. His Chosen People had rejected His Son. So now the Father was asking the Son to go redeem—buy back from Satan—the souls of men. He saw Jesus nodding in obedience and saying, "Yes, Father. But after I have accomplished this task, will you send the Holy Spirit to authenticate my work in the hearts of men—to make real to them this transaction made in their behalf, making known to them their opportunity to transfer from the kingdom of Satan into the Kingdom of God where they can receive forgiveness for their sins and experience redemption through the blood I will shed?"

He was astounded at how his imagination had run amuck, bringing thoughts and images to his mind, something he would hold dear but keep secret lest he be mistaken for a mystic and thought guilty of adding to the Scriptures. He was jolted because he knew the scenario as such was not in the Bible. His thought patterns kept rumbling. He knew he had been redeemed years ago when he surrendered at a Billy Graham Crusade, but at that time or even since then had he seriously considered how he had been purchased. The idea was just now taking hold. He wondered if the other prayer warriors were being dealt with in such a personal way. He supposed not, since they were able to participate and sing. His vocal cords just wouldn't function so he continued to listen and ponder.

The harmonizing had shifted from choruses to hymns. "On a hill far away stood an old rugged cross/ The emblem of suffering and shame/ And I love that old cross/ Where the dearest and best/ For a world of lost sinners was slain/ So I'll cherish the old rugged cross/ Till my trophies at last I lay down/ I will cling to the old rugged cross/ And exchange it some day for a crown." Another truth flooded his soul: Suddenly it dawned on him that of all the religions with their many deities making claims on the minds and emotions of people, Jesus Christ was the only one who had died for the benefit of mankind. Why, he wondered, didn't evangelists and pastors use that truth more often and more emphatically to bring misled and misguided people into the Kingdom? Well, maybe that truth had been and was being stressed, but people like himself were not registering the nugget as they should. Honesty forced him to admit that he was just now computing the fact for the first time.

Following that thought, his meandering mind began to slow down, and he realized the group had shifted to another old-time favorite: "What can wash away my sin?/ Nothing but the blood of Jesus/ What can make me whole again?/ Nothing but the blood of Jesus/ O precious is the flow/ That washes white as snow/ No other fount I know/ Nothing but the blood of Jesus."

On the third verse, he was able to join in, his rich baritone adding depth. He wondered when the prayers would start. Glancing at his luminous watch, he realized they had been there almost an hour. The wizards, or whatever one wanted to call them, were supposed to come on the scene in fifteen minutes, that is, if they showed at all. He had wondered all along if they were bluffing. Guess he'd learn shortly. He felt squeamish, but the doctor beside him was a comfort. He seemed to know more than the average person about some of these things. Why had the Corleys not spoken up? Maybe they had, but he, having been caught up in his own personal experience, had not heard them. Again he was reminded that his own heart had been punctured. Might the singing have a similar effect on the warlocks? He didn't know about the others, but he was getting more and more nervous. He wasn't exactly shaking, but his teeth were chattering, and his hands were clammy. Well, if the doctor didn't question the situation, he wouldn't either, but it was difficult to resist an inquiry. Surely the others were not as distracted as he, because somebody was bringing the power down, and he knew it wasn't Bill Dozier. His only worthwhile effort had been driving and parking the van. Now if he could just get this bunch safely back to the church.

He felt so non-spiritual. He found himself whispering, "Lord, bring me back to where I was a few minutes ago. I'm so schizo—taken up with You for a time and then taken away unto myself. Why don't they show up and let's get this over with? They tell me these are just kids—late teens mostly. Then why are men like me afraid of them? I suppose it's because they have the power of the devil in them, and that gives me a real spooky feeling. Well, the others may not be praying, just singing, but Lord, I'm asking You to protect me from these empowered devils—that is, if they are empowered, and they must be because they can sure get some people all screwed up. I'm asking You, Lord, to protect us all and to put these devilish emissaries on the run. And, Lord, I'm asking You to come down hard on them and cause them to give up their fascination with these sinful involvements and come to know You and get saved. I ask these things in the powerful name of Jesus."

He glanced again at his watch: 12:05. Only five minutes left. If the thugs didn't show in five minutes, should he go out and bring the van around for a quick pickup? Nobody had addressed all these questions now popping into his head. When he had previously raised some such related questions, the Corleys and the pastor would always obliquely say, "The Holy Spirit will lead." Well, it was time for some such leading.

The doctor was calm and collected, and apparently Ms. McVey was too. They just kept singing, and singing, and singing. Was he the only one in turmoil? "Lord," he said, "if this waiting continues, take me back to whatever I experienced shortly after I arrived. That was heavenly, but this is hell. I think I'm gonna be sick—I mean sick like, you know, barfing up. I never have quite known what my exact calling is, but I don't think it's setting captives free in a graveyard. When the Pastor and I scouted this place out the other morning I didn't have reservations. Maybe I should have so he could have picked somebody else in my place—somebody who could take it."

At that point, the words to "Nearer My God to Thee" got his attention, and as the verse came to a close, he heard the pastor say in his sanctuary voice, "Perfect love casts out fear." Oh, he thought, he's talking to me. I'm the only one afraid. But to his amazement something was happening to him again. Peace descended upon him. His teeth quit chattering. The rigidity was leaving his spine. He felt as though he was melting. "Oh Lord, I go from one extreme to another, but that's all right. Melting down is better than breaking apart like peanut brittle. Just keep it up. Maybe I won't have to barf after all."

At the end of the next verse, the singing stopped and a silence enveloped the entire cemetery. Not even an automobile was in transit. If the thugs were on the premises, he wondered how they had arrived, and if so, why they didn't get at whatever they were supposed to be getting at. Though he was still asking questions, the probing was much more serene. He was much more tranquil but still eager to get to the van and back to the church.

At that moment, several figures, walking in a straight line directly toward the corner of the cemetery, fanned out, every other one
going to the right and every other one to the left, cutting the corner
off from the rest of the cemetery by forming a quarter-circle around
it. The best he could tell, there appeared to be about a dozen of them.
Their heads were covered or draped with something that looked like
hoods. The action was deliberate and swift but not a sound was
made. Then from the mid-point of the arc came a call: "We are here.
Step forward, Selected One, and give your password. Prove your
allegiance to the ruler of all the dead and the living by proclaiming
him Magnifico."

From the very corner of the cemetery came a voice that sounded
like many voices in unison: "He who dwells in the secret place of the
Most High shall abide under the shadow of the Almighty. I will say
of the Lord, He is my Refuge and my Fortress, my God. He shall
cover thee with His feathers and under His wing shall thy trust. His
truth shall be thy shield and buckler."

From the left of the quarter-circle Bill heard a whimpering cry
and then a tiny squeal over toward the right. From the center sounded a voice of warning: "You have ten seconds to step forward, oh
Selected One."

This warning was countered with a voice Bill recognized as the
pastor's, "Be still; be still; and know that I am God." He could tell the
figures were struggling to move but weren't getting anywhere. The
voice emerged again. "Be still, and know that I am God." At that
command, they quit struggling and appeared to freeze. Then a heavenly harmony, all in unison, came cascading into his hearing.

"He is Lord/ He is Lord/ He has risen from the dead/ And He is
Lord/ Every knee shall bow/ Every tongue confess/ That Jesus Christ
is Lord."

Bill almost lost his breath. The three or four figures in his view
fell to their knees, and he was sure he heard sobs and moans. Had
the others done the same thing? And before he could ascertain further, he himself was on his knees. So were the doctor and Ms. McVey.
The singing continued. He thought he heard them quoting the
phrases along with the singers. He was not mistaken. They were crying, and between sobs trying to repeat the chorus.

Then the intercessors, led by the Corleys, softly sang, "There is a
fountain filled with blood/ Drawn from Emanuel's veins/ and sinners plunged beneath that flood/ Lose all their guilty stains/ Lose all

their guilty s-t-a-i-n-s/ Lose all their guilty stains/ And sinners plunged beneath that flood/ Lose all their guilty stains."

The refrain was repeated several times then ceased. The silence was deafening. Then a voice, apparently from the leader who had issued the other orders, very calmly inquired, "What shall we do? What shall we do?"

The answer was immediate. "You must renounce your allegiance to Satan and accept Jesus as your Lord. Go your way, and the Blessed Holy Spirit will direct each of you to places of worship where you will find salvation for your souls. Return not to that sinful habitation from which you came but return each of you to the home of your parents. Confess your ties to the demonic and satanic as grievous sins. Release Sonny Houston and all the others you have been holding captive. You may leave now, and God have mercy on your souls. Again, I say, each of you go home to your parents. God will guide and provide directions. Amen."

* * *

Again it was Sunday lunch for Weeda and Kyle at Westwinds. They had ordered and were waiting. It had gotten to be a habit—ordering the same thing. For health's sake, they were eating more and more fish. Today it was breaded halibut, buttered brown rice, glazed carrots, and slaw. They sat talking and enjoying their appetizers of stuffed mushrooms.

"Well, my dear, it has been more than a month now since that soul-shaking experience at Sunset," said Kyle.

"I know, and it's still unbelievable—all that happened that night to say nothing of what has transpired since."

"It just goes to show what concerted prayer can bring to pass. I shudder to think how many of us will be ashamed at the Judgment Seat of Christ when we realize what failed to be accomplished because we neglected to pray. I, for one, don't do enough, but I'm working toward improvement. Are things still working out for Sonny?"

"They are. He's trying to catch up on his assignments. By going to summer school, he'll be able to graduate in August, but his GPA will probably be in the C range, and that'll limit his choice of colleges."

"But the fact that he has gotten turned around is miraculous. The going has been real rough for Cody, I understand."

"True, but he's so grateful about what's happening with Sonny that he's not complaining about the downturns in his business and social life. Says he's willing to suffer the losses, that even though his business is suffering, it's a small price to pay for what he has gained in coming to know Christ. He and Anna are sensing some rejection at the church and are thinking of moving their membership to Hilltop Community."

"Very good idea. He's a survivor. He'll weather the storm. More good reports keep coming in as a result of all that intercession. Corley called just before I left to pick you up, saying they are now scheduled to counsel with the ringleader of that coven Sonny was caught up in. He said Pastor Savage is beside himself over what's happening. Says the two covens are breaking up altogether. This is something that man has been praying about for two or three years. He's still faithfully holding those prayer sessions and is training another group now. Great rewards will be awaiting him at that Judgment Seat."

Throughout the meal they continued to delight themselves over the outcome of the Wednesday night experience in the cemetery.

As Kyle was paying the check, he asked, "What are you doing this afternoon? Anything that can't wait?"

"I don't think so. Why?"

"I'd like you to take a ride with me. There's something I want to show you. Maybe you can advise me."

"Sure. I don't know about the advice, but I'd like the ride. What are you showing off?"

"I'll let that wait for now."

* * *

"Kyle, I can't imagine what you could possibly want to show me in this area of town. If you keep driving, we'll soon be out in the country. Don't tell me your medical group is thinking of relocating?"

"Hardly. Anyway, all this area is restricted residential."

"And so beautiful—such lovely homes."

"Easy on the eyes, aren't they?"

With that comment, he pulled into a driveway, parked very near the entrance, quickly went around and opened the door for Weeda. "Let's go in and look around."

"Sure, but—"

"Don't ask questions. Just look."

The house was a modified Colonial reused brick structure situated on a rising knoll. Four maples were well established and rightly spaced at the corners, not blocking the view of the entrance from the street. Kyle turned the key to the front door, and they entered the foyer where Kyle stopped and started explaining himself.

"Weeda, I'm thinking of buying this place. I like my apartment, but some unsavory characters are beginning to move in, and I need to get out before I—well, I just need to make a move. Look around and tell me what you think. You have good taste and a practical mind. I need your input."

"Sure, but—"

"Just look around. There are three bedrooms, three baths, this large living-formal dining combo, which I think measures about thirty by eighteen. There's a large den with a fireplace. The kitchen has a dining nook, also a grill area, and there's a two-car garage. You'll see that the backyard is not much but the potential is great. Anyway, let's look and afterwards you give me your candid opinion."

They walked around. Kyle was cool and business-like, but Weeda was puzzled. She had never seen him so utterly taken up with himself, so seemingly consumed with his own desires and needs, but then she could understand. He was an extremely successful physician, and most people in his profession were not living in apartments. So why should he? After they had surveyed the house and grounds for at least an hour, they carne back to the kitchen counter where Kyle took some paper cups from the cabinet, and they quenched their thirst with tepid tap water. He set his cup down and facing her asked. "What do you think—an honest assessment? The house is five years old. The family is selling because they have been transferred with a growing company. I need to give the owner an answer by Wednesday. The price is not out of bounds for this area. What's your advice?"

"I think you've already set your heart on it. You'll enjoy living here."

"Now what about you? Would you like living here?"

"Sure. It's many notches above my little townhouse, but—"

"It's very important to me that you like it, because I think it's time we take up residence together."

"Are you asking me to—?"

"Yes, I'm asking you to marry me. Our moral ethics dictate marriage, not a shacking up arrangement. Right?"

She was in his arms. He kissed her long and tenderly, then said, "I don't know your wishes concerning the wedding. I'll go along with whatever is dear and important to you, but I do have a couple of suggestions."

"Yes, I'm eager to hear them."

"I picked out the house. Now I'd like you to select your ring— about a two carat—and it would please me if you'd take the lead in furnishing this domicile. But my main request is that we not put off the wedding ceremony lest you get caught up in another Sonny-like situation. Also, I would hope you could be contented come September with managing a home and managing me. Would you like that?"

"Very much, very much, very much. And I have a suggestion."

"I'm listening."

"Could we get married by Pastor Savage in his church?"

"No problem. And why don't we consider doing what the Houstons are doing—moving our membership there?"

She didn't answer. His lips had hers fully engaged.

Printed in the United States
19390LVS00003B/106-126